T0198620

Circles

Circles

Blondie

iUniverse, Inc.
New York   Bloomington

Circles

Copyright © 2006, 2009 by Blondie

All rights reserved. No part of this book may be used or reproduced by any means, graphic, electronic, or mechanical, including photocopying, recording, taping or by any information storage retrieval system without the written permission of the publisher except in the case of brief quotations embodied in critical articles and reviews.

This is a work of fiction. All of the characters, names, incidents, organizations, and dialogue in this novel are either the products of the author's imagination or are used fictitiously.

iUniverse books may be ordered through booksellers or by contacting:

iUniverse
1663 Liberty Drive
Bloomington, IN 47403
www.iuniverse.com
1-800-Authors (1-800-288-4677)

Because of the dynamic nature of the Internet, any Web addresses or links contained in this book may have changed since publication and may no longer be valid. The views expressed in this work are solely those of the author and do not necessarily reflect the views of the publisher, and the publisher hereby disclaims any responsibility for them.

ISBN: 978-1-4401-8995-1 (sc)
ISBN: 978-1-4401-8997-5 (dj)
ISBN: 978-1-4401-8996-8 (ebook)

Printed in the United States of America

iUniverse rev. date: 11/25/2009

Acknowledgments

First and foremost I would like to thank God, because without his grace and mercy nothing I do would be possible. I have had quite a rough time this year, and this is really my dream coming true. I wrote these two stories almost three years ago, and at times I just felt like giving up, throwing in the towel and saying I'm through with writing. Of course I wasn't through with it, and that is why you're reading my work today. God is so good, and I am the living proof.

I want to thank my mother Marie Del'Rio Roberts, but better known as Del to everyone in my family. Without you there would have been no me, and I love you for that with all of my heart. You have always been my mother and my father, and as I grew older and wiser you became my friend. You tell me like it is, whether I want to hear it from you or not. You're always there when I need you, and you always have my best interest at heart You are the best mother that anyone could ever have, and I am blessed with your love daily. I know sometimes we get caught up in our lives, and we may forget to say this simple phrase. So for every time that I forget to say it, I LOVE YOU MOMMY.

To my older sisters Linda, Asia, and Towana. You have all played a tremendous part in the making of this book, and I will never forget all of your help. Linda was there from day one, back in 2006 when I said I was going to write a book she always believed that I could do it. She cheered me on, and never gave up hope that my book was going to come out even when we weren't on good terms. So from youngest sister to oldest sister, thank you Mecca, and I love you. Asia believed in me so much that she gave me some financial help, when I was so close to my dream that I could touch it, but my funds were a little low, and I didn't know what I would do. My big sister came through for me like she always does, and for that Black Betty I love you and appreciate you.

Towana and her close friend Elisha asked to read my book Circles right after I finished writing it in 2006, and let me tell you it was a mess. I had never wrote a book before in my life, and everything was wrong with it. But not to them, they told me Circles was one of the best stories that they had ever read. So if it wasn't for their praise about the book, maybe it wouldn't even be out today. Thanks Trixie, and Elisha, I love you guys. To my neighbor Boobi you keep me grounded, and when I lose my cool you always have my back. I love you, and thank you for all of your support. To Joelle it's eleven years later, and yes we're still standing I love you bitch. Annie and Lorena we have been friends forever, and we haven't always seen eye to eye. But throughout everything that we have been through over the years I love you crazy bitches to death. Shawn thanks for your advice, when I needed a clear head you were there for me, and I love you for that

I want to gave a huge shout out to my oldest brother Daryl Roland Barnes, he know that I could do it, and I love him for that. I did it big bro. thanks for all of your support. Not to leave out my other siblings, you know who you are. I love you, and I appreciate all of your support and love. Get ready because I'm here to stay, I told you Blondie was coming, and there is no stopping me. To my friend Chocolate you were there from the start of my book Circles, and you probably thought that I forget about you and your little man. Its always love baby girl, and thank you for all of your support .To my jersey girl Bee, I finally did it. I love you, and thank you for all of your support.

To my friend Delaine who never stopped asking when was my book was coming out, so she could tell the whole job. Laine it's finally here, so please spread the word. To my First Ladies from Foster projects, I love you'll bitches. I'm a First Lady for life, can you feel me. To my childhood friends from Saint Nicholas projects, where both books you are about to read are based out of. I love you all, and just because I'm not living there doesn't mean that I forget about you   Life is to short, and I want to live mine's to the fullest. I'm not taking anything for granted anymore, and just the fact that my book is out now is proof that it wasn't all for nothing. To my nieces and nephew, I finally did it. I love you guys, and thanks for your support.

Last but not the least I want to thank my son Armani, we have had a rough time this year Slim but we stayed strong together. No mother wants to feel like she is failing her child, and there were times due to our circumstances that I felt that way. I was wrong for feeling like that, and my son told me so. One day a few months back we had a heart to heart talk about life, and both of us expressed how we were feeling. I told Armani that I felt like a bad mother, and I explained to him why I was feeling that way. Armani looked at me and said, you could never be a bad mother because you treat me so good. He then went on to say that he could never imagine having anyone else as his mother, and that he appreciated me.

He told me that he loved me so much, and that he always would. So when I feel sad all I have to do is think about what my son said to me, and his words always makes me feel better. I want to leave you with a phrase that I once read, which inspired me. The victory isn't in getting published, the victory is in actually getting the book finished. If I forgot to mention anyone, please don't take it personal. I'm just so excited.

In Memory

I dedicate this book to my dad, Verdell Gordon. You were taken from us to soon, and your children miss you dearly. We will never have another father, but we know that you made it into heaven's pearly gates. So with this knowledge we know that we will see you again in the future, until we see you again daddy keep smiling like you always did when you were here with us. We love you daddy, and we miss you so much.

In loving memory to Jaynard Dwight Mabry, and to all the little angels that were taken from us to soon. You are truly missed, and you will never be forgotten. You floated away on the wings of a dove, but we know that you know nothing but everlasting love. Rest in peace little ones.

A Crazy Harlem Dream

A Short Story

Introduction

Hello, my name is Tasha Heart, and this is my tragic story. All my life I have dreamed of being married with a sexy and supportive husband. We would have three gorgeous children—two boys and a little girl. We would all live happily ever after in a two-family house with a white picket fence in the suburbs. We would have a little black dog named Tiger and money to last us a lifetime. But I come from the mean streets of Harlem, and not all of our dreams come true.

Chapter One

My life was in no way perfect, but it could have been far worse. My mother, Gloria Janice Heart, was a hardworking, strong black woman who would do anything for any one of her three children. There was Danny, my twenty-one-year-old brother, Karen, my seventeen-year-old sister, and myself. My name is Tasha, and I am the baby of the family at age sixteen.

It was only the four of us living together, but it wasn't always like this. It happened because our father, Gerald Heart, had been missing for the last four and a half years. He went to work one morning, like it was a normal day, and just never returned home. He was a truck driver for an Italian trucking company out in New Jersey. That company only dealt with trips out of state, so my dad was gone quite a bit.

Sometimes he would be gone weeks and weeks at a time. He said there was big money to be made out there, and he was going to be the one to make it. Plus he really loved driving those big trucks around the world. Ever since my dad's disappearance, life has been real hard for us, and money has been very scarce. When my dad was around, we never had to want for anything, but now with only one income in our home times were rough.

My mother had three growing kids to feed, and we were always growing out of our clothes. Her money was not stretching that far and shit was tight. My mom worked at Mount Sinai Hospital on One Hundredth Street and Madison Avenue. She was a nurse and had been working there for the last ten years. She made a pretty penny doing the job she loved. However, I could tell that life was overwhelming for her, and eventually she would come crashing down.

Now Danny was at the age where he thought he was the sexiest thing alive. And he thought that he was a full-fledged pimp. Girls called our house all day and night, and if Danny wasn't home, he wanted you to take a message. Like he was a king, and we were his peasants. As for Karen,

1

she wanted to become a doctor, so school was very important to her, and homegirl did not play around with her studies.

All I did was dream and remember better days. My imagination was wild, and I could invent a story in a matter of seconds. People really believed me when I relayed my far-out tales. Sometimes, when I got carried away, I even thought that they were true. But we will get more into my thoughts later on in the story. As for my mother, she had no life outside of her family and work, but she always tried to have a smile on her face.

I knew that she was hurting inside over not knowing if my father was dead or alive. And the damn police had no new leads to investigate, none at all, and when they did catch a whiff of what might have happened to my father it would always turn into a dead end. They told my mother that as far as they could see, my daddy just ran away. My mother did not believe that bullshit for one second, and she told the detectives so. "Gerald loved this family more than life itself, and if he were running away from something he would have taken us with him."

Then the nasty white detective looked up at her, and with a slight smirk on his face said, "Not if he was running away from you." That comment left my mother stunned; there was nothing left to say. The state would not declare him legally dead until seven years had passed, so all we could do was pray and wait for a miracle. Life has gone on for the last four years, and thankfully we were making it. Until February 2, 2005. On that horrible day, something awful would change our lives forever.

Karen and I went to different high schools. She went to a school out in Queens and I went to Norman Thomas in lower Manhattan. Danny was in John Jay College of Criminal Justice, and since my mother was always at work, he was our babysitter. She made sure that Danny came straight home from school to watch over Karen and me until she got in. My mother came home from the hospital usually around seven o'clock in the evening, and she was always tired. She was always very protective of us girls, but now even more so with my father gone.

On the evening of February 2, my mother never came home. We all just thought that she had to work late and just forget to call home. It was no sweat, though. Danny cooked his specialty for dinner—franks and beans over white rice. Then we all did our homework, took our showers, and got ready for bed. As usual when bedtime rolled around, the fake pimp was still on the telephone. He did not care what time it was; he was laying his mack game down on them hoes. But all I knew was he better be in the bed by the time Mama came home, or his ass would be grass.

The next morning Karen woke me up and told me to get ready for school. I asked her if Mama had come home. She looked at me, and said no. She thought Mama was still at work, and she would be here by the time we came from school. Something about her expression scared me though, and all day at school I was worried.

For the life of me, I could not concentrate on my schoolwork or anything thing else for that matter. My thoughts were so scrambled. All I wanted to do was to get home and see my mother's sweet face. The day just seemed to drag on, and I could not wait until three o'clock so I could get the hell out of the classroom. At last I heard the dismissal bell ring. When school let out, I walked to the train station for my ride uptown. When I got to my stop on 135th Street I walked the four blocks to my street, turned the corner, and that is when I saw the police car in front of my building.

At that moment I knew in my heart that I would never see my mother alive again. The police told us that there had been a terrible accident on 104th Street and Madison Avenue. Our mother was in a three-car pileup, and she died at the scene. It took them awhile to confirm the fatalities so that is why we did not know sooner. Right away Karen and I burst into tears. I guess Danny was trying to be strong for our sakes because he stood up tall and held his head high. He never shed a tear while we were grieving.

The next few days seemed to spin around us. Arrangements had to be made, people had to be notified, and now we were all alone in the world. With no mother and no father, we did not have much family left that we knew of. My mother was an only child and both her parents had been dead for years, and my father's parents had never liked my mother. They always thought that she was not good enough for my father, so that meant when we were born we were never good enough for him either. My father only had one younger brother, Gary, who we saw quite a lot when we were younger, but ever since my father disappeared so did our uncle Gary.

They were very close brothers, and Uncle Gary could not handle the fact that my father had vanished without a trace. My siblings and I all seemed to be in a deep trance, so thank God for our neighbors. We had lived at 230 West 131st Street in apartment 2G for so long that everyone around the area knew our family, and everyone offered us their help. We knew Mama had life insurance and Danny knew where the policy was. Our neighbor, Mrs. Clinton, took Danny to Unity Funeral Home on 126th Street and Eighth Avenue to make all the preparations.

Karen and I could not go back to school. I am not even sure if we ate or slept those first few days after her death. We moved around like zombies. No one talked or showed much emotion besides us girls crying periodically, and Danny did not even do that. I was worried about him because he was acting so tough, and I knew he was in pain just as we were, but he told us not to worry about him. He said that he could handle anything and that we would survive this. Thank God Danny was old enough to keep the apartment and get custody of us, and that is just what he did.

Danny stepped up and became our guardian, our provider, he became our everything. The day of our mother's funeral it was pouring outside and very dark, which matched our moods. Our mother was laid out in a smoked gray casket, and she had on a flowing white gown with her hair spread out all around her. There were so many flowers in the funeral home, and we received so many sympathy cards. Everyone she knew came out and paid their last respects, coworkers from her job, and patients she had treated. It felt so stuffy in the church I couldn't breathe, and I couldn't wait until Gloria Janice Heart would be laid to rest at last.

As soon as the funeral started, the preacher had everyone in tears, and when it was over my mother was buried in Wood Lawn Cemetery out in New Jersey. All the neighbors cooked for the wake, so we had more than enough food but none of us could eat. We all just sat close together on the couch, drawing from each other's sorrow. All I wanted was for this day to end. When the last person finally left our house at twelve midnight, our home was spotless. Mrs. Clinton, our next-door neighbor, and Mrs. Brown from the fifth floor put all the food away. They swept and mopped the floor and Mr. Brown took out the garbage.

For the next two days Karen and I just sat in the living room side-by-side. We stared at the blank television screen not saying a word, until finally Danny said we had to stop this and pull ourselves together. He said next week we were all going back to school, and he was going to find a part-time job to earn some extra money.

He looked at us and said, "You both know that Mommy would not want us falling apart like this. She would want us to be strong and survive, and that is just what we will try to do."

I didn't know about Karen or Danny, but I was sick of being depressed. I was ready to try to live a normal life without my mother around, but inside I was afraid that I would not make it. The next week we tried to act as normal as possible under the circumstances, but it was so hard. That following Monday we all went back to school, and my first day back was rough.

Everyone kept apologizing and saying how sorry they were, but I just wished everyone would shut up and leave me the hell alone. The worst question was, "Is there anything we could do?" If they could not bring my mother back from the dead, why would they ask that stupid question? I just wanted to crawl under a rock and die! That day I ate lunch by myself, and just prayed that the rest of the day would fly by.

At three o'clock I rode the train uptown, and I walked home alone, lost in my thoughts. I bumped into Jackie. She was one of Karen's friends, and a real hot tamale. She said, "Hi Tasha," and before I could answer her, she asked me where Karen was. "I saw you two leave the building this morning, but when I got to school she wasn't there," she said.

"I don't know where Karen is, maybe she made herself invisible like I want to do," I said. "Now Jackie, I have to go," I said, and kept on walking. When I got home, Danny asked me how my day was. I looked at him, and said, "Dull! Danny, everybody just kept talking to me about Mama, and I just wanted them to leave me alone."

Danny led me to the couch, sat me down, and said, "Don't worry, kiddo, they will forget all about this real soon."

Then I put my head down, and said, "Yeah I know they will, but I won't."

We both sat there quite for a while until Danny told me that he had some good news, he had found a job.

"That's great," I said. "Where is it at?"

He told me his new job was at The Home Depot, and it paid ten dollars an hour. With his check, Mama's pension check, and me and Karen's SSI check, we would be taken care of. Money was not a problem any longer.

After our talk, Danny went to cook dinner while I completed my homework. Karen came home at seven thirty that night and Danny asked her, "Where have you been?"

"Out," she said, and went straight to her room, and slammed the door closed. At that point, I knew something was wrong with her, because Karen never stayed out late. I followed her and knocked on her door.

When she didn't answer, I opened her door, and walked right in. She was changing her clothes, and on her breasts were bite marks.

I closed the door and asked, "Oh, Karen, who did that to you?"

She looked at me and said, "I will tell you if you promise not to say anything."

"Karen, I promise, now give me the dirt."

She looked at me, and then said, "Okay, I'll tell you. His name is Tommy Hopkins, and he lives on 143rd Street and Eighth Avenue."

"Where do you know him from?"

"From school, dummy! Now shut up or I won't finish telling you." She continued, "Tommy always liked me, and I don't know I guess today he knew I needed a friend. Today was the first time that I went to his house. We cut school and went straight there this morning. Tommy's mom was at work, only his twin brother Johnny and his homeboys were there because they always cut class.

"We went right to Tommy's room and watched television, and a little while later Johnny knocked on the door. When he opened the door all of a sudden, I smelled something sweet, and it smelled very good. I asked what was that smell, Tommy said weed. Then he asked me if I wanted to try it. I thought about it, and then I said sure, why not? The first pull was a killer but after Tommy taught me how to hold my smoke in and blow it out right I was good to go.

"After we smoked two more blunts, Tommy started rubbing on my breasts, and it felt very good. I asked him if I could touch him. He said, 'Hell yes you can touch me,' and then he pulled off his sweatshirt. He opened up his pants, and then he pulled his dick out."

I was mesmerized by the story I was hearing. I could not believe that Karen had seen a real dick up close and personal. My mother had us so sheltered all of our lives, and I had so many questions that I wanted answered but I stayed quiet and let Karen finish telling her story.

"Tommy put my hand on his penis, and told me to rub it up and down. Then the next thing I knew he started making all kinds of weird sounds, and sweat was running down his face. Then he told me to take off my pants, we laid down and he took off his boxers and my panties and bra. He started sucking on my breasts and sticking his fingers inside of me. That shit kind of hurt, but I didn't tell him to stop.

"Then all of a sudden, my pussy was very wet, and I wanted to feel him inside of me. I told him to put his dick in me, he looked at me and asked if I sure that I wanted to do this. I said I was sure, but he had to put a condom on first. He found one in his dresser drawer put it on, and then he guided his dick into me. Tasha, at first it was very painful, so painful that it brought tears to my eyes. But after about five pumps in and out the feeling changed, and it started feeling very good."

I had to interrupt her at that point, "It must not have felt that good if you were crying."

Karen looked at me, rolled her eyes, and said, "Tasha, it felt real good. I have never felt my pussy that wet before. Tash, it was dripping wet, and Tommy was banging my shit real hard. Then he yelled out, 'Karen, I'm coming, oh God I'm coming!' Then I felt something gushing out of his penis, and then he collapsed on top of me."

Karen was smiling like that was the best feeling, in the whole wide world. But I just didn't understand it, because I was still a virgin. After her story was done we went to the kitchen for dinner. Danny must have felt that something was up with Karen. All throughout dinner he kept asking her questions about her day, and he was staring at her.

I was quiet most of the meal. All that was on my mind was what Karen had told me about her first sexual experience. I needed that same feeling—now where did that thought come from? My thoughts scared the shit out me, but that's what happens when everybody around you is having sex. Then they tell you about it, only making your cravings worse.

After Karen's first sex act she started to act real different. Danny tried to keep a close watch on her, and Karen tried to keep a closer watch on Tommy. For some reason Tommy didn't want to be seen around town with Karen in public. And this being her first real boyfriend, she was not happy about how he was acting. She thought they were a couple and in love, and she wanted everyone to know about her new boo. Everyone that is except Danny. All I wanted was to hear more about her sex life. I was very horny most days, and extremely depressed the rest of the time.

We had all settled into our new home life, and we were just trying to make it. Since Danny was the sole provider of our family now, that meant that he was in charge of us. Whatever Danny wanted Danny usually got, and we really had no say in the matter. He was even tougher to live with than our mother was, and she always went overboard with her shit. Damn, I missed her so much sometimes I felt like I was suffocating.

Then just like that, the feeling went away. I knew it was anxiety, so I just prayed that it would go away. I really did not care how crazy Danny acted but Karen felt like she was grown, and she wasn't listening to anyone. Unknown to us, Karen hadn't been to school in the last month. This was her last year of high school and she was messing up. I knew some shit was about to hit the fan, and I was right.

When I got home from school one Monday, Danny was in a rage. He was cursing up a storm, and walking up and down the hallway saying, "When Karen gets home, her ass is mine!"

I asked him what happened, and then he showed me the letter from her school, asking that a parent or guardian come in for a conference. All I could do was hand the letters back to him, head to my room, and wait for the drama to unfold.

Two hours later I heard the front door open, then close, and then I heard Danny flipping out. He was yelling at Karen, asking her, "Where the fuck have you been, and why haven't you been going to school?"

I was nervous as I cracked my bedroom door open to watch the action.

I heard Karen say, "Look, Danny, I don't need this shit right now. I'm tired and I just want to go and lay down, can we talk about this later?"

Danny yelled, "Hell no, we have to talk about this shit right now!" Then he looked at her and said, "What the hell is wrong with your eyes and why do you keep moving around and shit?" Then he started screaming, "Karen, look at me!" When she did, Danny looked like he was going to be sick on the spot. At that moment all was quiet. He looked down the hall at me, and when he turned back to Karen he said, "Karen, what drug are you on?"

With an evil look in her eye, she said, "Danny, please, not right now," and pushed past him.

Danny grabbed Karen by her neck, threw her on the wall, pulled her head back, and looked deep into her eyes. He said, "Sis, how long have you been using cocaine?" Karen jerked away from him and ran in her room, slamming her door without giving him an answer. Danny looked back at me with tears in his eyes, and then he turned and walked into his room and closed his door. I was left standing there all alone with my thoughts. All I wanted was for everything to go back to the way it was before my father disappeared.

Chapter Two

Over the next couple of months nobody in my family really spoke to each other. That meant that I had a whole lot of time to do what I did best, dream. This time around I decided to put it down on paper. Instead of writing stories down each day like I did when I was younger, I now wrote poetry. Summing up my feelings in a few short lines made me feel good inside. Danny hardly came home anymore, I guess he was running from something in our home. After the incident with our sister he had changed in a very big way, and that left no room for anyone or anything. I think he felt like he failed Karen. I didn't agree—she made the choice to use drugs not him.

Danny was always very secretive and now it was ten times worse. He would not talk to me about anything. And Karen came home even less; basically she had moved out of our home and moved in with Tommy and his family.

When I asked her how his parents felt about her living there, she said, "Well, Tommy and Johnny don't know their father, and his mother has a boyfriend, so she stays with him most of the time. So in all actuality the apartment is ours, all Mrs. Hopkins does is pay the rent."

We had that discussion on the day when she came and got the rest of her clothes, and that was three weeks ago. In all that time I only saw Danny five times, so if you asked me I was living alone and loving it. I guess my imagination was far out there, because in class we had to write a story for English class. When I read mine to the class everyone was sitting in total shock, even Mrs. Stevenson, my fourth period teacher. The story was about poverty and despair, with a lot of hopelessness and misery. Everything was going good until I read the ending part, which was the poem.

Knowledge

Living in the ghetto
Middle class slum

That's what they say
Wanting to become something

But there's always something in your way

Wanting to move forward
But always looking back

In God we trust
He holds the key for most

But we can't forget the devil
He comes like a cloud of smoke

Tearing apart families
Doing evil things to us
Taking away our dreams

And planting his seeds in all of us

We can fight him
The church people always say

We can tear him down
But can we really?

Who is there to show us the way?

That's when you get down on your knees
And look up above and call on the Lord's name

So our father can show us
The wings of a dove

Then you hear a voice speak

It says you're never really alone
I'm always on your side

And with this newfound knowledge you will survive

When I said the last word and looked up at the class, I didn't see a closed mouth in the room. After Mrs. Stevenson pulled herself together, she made the class stand up and clap for me. I didn't understand why she was making a big thing out of my story, but after class Mrs. Stevenson asked me to stay for a little while longer.

When everyone else was gone, she explained to me what she was feeling.

She took my hands into hers and said, "Tasha, I grew up in poverty too, far from where I am today. Look at me, I made it." Then she told me that I had a gift, and she knew it would only get better with time. She told me my story was good but my poem was inspirational, and she said at one point in her life she felt the same way. But she always remembered that God was good and he always had her back.

She told me to never give up hope, and to keep on writing then she told me to have a good night, and to get home safe. I ran all the way from the train station to my block, even more excited about my newfound talent. But Danny sidetracked me. He was sitting in the kitchen waiting for me when I got home. Danny looked real tired, and I thought he would stay for a while.

But when I asked him where he had been staying, he snapped at me and said, "None of your damn business." Then he told me there was food in the refrigerator, threw me a couple of dollars, and walked out the front door.

Hell, he didn't even say goodbye, and once again I was left alone, but my writing would see me through. Now I had a few friends in school that I hung out with, but Candy was my number one girl. She lived right around the corner from me on 8th avenue. We also hung out with Tiny, Squeak, and Honey. Of course these were their nicknames. I had one too—it was Te Te. This was my crew, and these broads were always down for whatever. People knew not to fuck with us. I had not hung out with them since my mother's death, but I was slowly bouncing back.

One day Candy did not come to school. When we spoke the night before she sounded fine. But I knew her stepfather, Eddie, was a mean son of a bitch, and he and Candy did not get along at all, so I hoped everything was all right. From lunchtime until three o'clock I called Candy's phone, but she didn't answer. At the end of the school day we were all worried, so we went uptown together and walked to her building. Just like the day when my mother died, there were cops everywhere.

When we reached her building, Tiny wondered out loud what happened, and one of Candy's nosy-ass neighbors told us what went down.

"Eddie had been beating Candy's mother, and when Candy went to help her Eddie beat her unconscious."

I asked what happened to Candy's mother, and the nosy lady said she was dead by the time the ambulance arrived. Ms. Nosy said that they rushed Candy to Harlem hospital, and they were not sure that she was going to make it. We were all devastated. I walked off, and asked one of the police officers if I could go inside to get Candy some clothes to take to the hospital.

He looked at me for a second, and then he asked me who I was to the family, and I replied that I was Candy's cousin. He looked at me again and told me it was very ugly inside, but if I could handle it to go ahead. Then he stepped aside and allowed me to enter her home. The house was in shambles, and there was blood everywhere and on everything. All I could do was say a little prayer, and then I grabbed a few of Candy's items and left. When we reached the hospital we were told that Candice Ramos could only have two visitors at a time, and only for a short while. The four of us took turns.

When I first entered her room I didn't know how she was going to look, and mentally I prepared myself for the worst. But surprisingly she only had one nasty cut over her right eye. Other than that mark she looked like she was asleep. My girls and I rotated shifts until visiting hours were over at 8:00 PM, and then we all kissed Candy's cheek and got ready to go home. I left Candy's clothes with the nurse, and I told her that we would be back the next afternoon. We were all very depressed, and the walk from the hospital was extremely quiet. We did not know what to say to each other, so we said nothing instead. When we got to our block we all said goodnight and went upstairs to get ready for school the next day. That night I tried to go right to sleep but I couldn't. So I got out my notebook and wrote a poem for my homegirl.

Friendship

Friends are supposed to be there through thick and thin
But through the fights who will win?
You'll lose someone you love

All because of something that was said
And the next thing you know your friendship is dead

Saying evil things
Just to make someone feel mad
And then all of a sudden
Inside you're feeling sad

Because you hurt someone you love
Who you cherish
And who you understand
But now all that's gone
Your friendship has blown away just like the sand

All you wish for is that things could be the same
And for you to no longer be in shame
And maybe God will take away your pain
All you do is let your tears mingle with the rain
So if you have a real friend, who you know will never
    let you down
Hold on to that special someone, because good friends
    are like standing on solid ground

After I wrote that poem I felt a little bit better, because there were many females in our neighborhood and at school who fought over the littlest things. Friends stealing friends boyfriends, or friends talking shit about each other behind their backs. If you can fuck over someone you call your friend, then you are really not their friend. I mean, it's bad enough that the school is so big, so of course everyone is always in everyone else's business, but I'm just happy that has never happened to me and my crew. Shit, I've seen a lot of friendships break up over the nonsense I just wrote about, but I know that will never be us. I can only hope it won't happen—but I have seen stranger things.

Two weeks had passed and there was still no movement from Candy, but the doctors were very optimistic about her recovery. They were not ready to give up hope, and neither were we. The Crimeez, as we called ourselves, were always by her side. There was no money to bury Ms. Ramos and no family to claim her body, so of course the city buried her in a potter's field. I wondered how Candy would handle that news when she woke up, if she woke up. All we could do was be there for her and try to help her through this fucked-up time.

I had moved all of Candy's clothes to my house, and when Danny came home for a visit I told him that she was moving in. He shrugged his shoulders and said that he didn't care, and then he gave me some money and said he would see me next week. I was dying to know where Danny was staying, and what he was doing. But I knew not to ask him any questions, since the last time he got all crazy on me. The police had no leads on Eddie's whereabouts, but they said that he couldn't hide forever, and when he resurfaced they would grab him and put him away for life.

And where was Karen? The last time I saw her was when she came and got her clothes, which was over a month ago. I was really starting to get worried about her. It just seemed like my family was going in so many different directions, and there was no one to pull us together. I was only making it because of my writing, but what about the others? What was holding them together?

Two days later Honey and Squeak said they were going to see a man about a dog, as they called it. That saying meant mind your business, and stay out of ours. Those two had gotten real secretive lately, and I wanted to know why. But Tiny and I were on our way to the hospital so those sluts were lucky for now, I would have to question them later on. When we got to the hospital, Nurse Thomas had some good news for us. Candy had finally opened her eyes.

"Candice opened her eyes at 11:30 AM. We called your cell phones—why were they off?" she asked.

I had to laugh because she was being very nosy, but I liked her so it was cool. I told her that during school hours we didn't want any distractions, so we kept them off until school let out. She smiled, pinched my cheek, and said, "That's nice." Like your grandmother or somebody older would do. Then she walked us to Candy's room.

When we got to Miss Thing's room she was sitting up in bed watching television and looking pissed off. We walked over to her, gave her a hug and a kiss, and then I asked her what was wrong.

She looked at me and said, "Te, where is my mother? Why isn't she here? Why isn't she here Te?" What could I tell her? Only the whole truth would do. We each sat on one side of her bed, took her hands in ours, and then I told her that her mother was dead.

I told her everything I knew about that day her mother was murdered, and then we just held her while she cried. We sat there until we heard visiting hours were over. We didn't want to leave her, but what could we do? So we said goodnight, and told her we would be there early the next morning to see her. She didn't blink or say a word. I didn't like the look in her eyes but we had to go, because the evening nurses were on our ass.

That night my dreams were filled with sorrow and dread and I knew something big was about to happen. Call it woman's intuition or whatever you like, but shit was about to hit the fan. The next morning I wrote a poem called Feelings, and once I got the words down on paper I felt more relaxed and carefree for the moment.

Feelings

As I lay in my bed
Awaiting the light of day to come
All my feelings and emotions
Came rushing at me all at once

I sit back and think
About everything that makes me weep
Crying, some people say that's the answer
But for me writing is more enhancing

It clears my mind
It touches my soul
Writing how I feel
I can be so bold
The winds stand still
My mind floats away
The words start to flow out
Not caring what others would say

Expressing myself so the world can tell
Even someone with as many problems as me
Can separate hurt and pain from reality
Letting other's know
That there's always someplace to go
To be alone and just feel free

Writing is my gift
So if you have a gift, use it well

And let God guide you
From this living hell

The pain will not always be there
It will disappear soon enough
This I know is true, because in God I know we trust
Do not shed a tear, at times just completely let yourself
    go
Your feelings are your feelings, and no one but you can
    ever stop your growth

Chapter Three

When I got to the hospital the next day the gang was already there, so I sat down on the bed for a little girl talk. Candy was just lying very still, while everyone else talked around her. My curiosity was getting the best of me, so I turned to Squeak and Honey and asked them why they had been keeping secrets from us and what were the two of them into. They both looked speechless and of course Squeak, with her punk ass, put her head down.

That bitch Honey had the nerve to ask me, "What is it to you?"

I said, "The Crimeez don't keep secrets, we are one for all and all for one, now answer the fucking question, Honey." I looked between those two sluts to see which one would open up their mouth first, and once again it was Honey.

"If you must know, we are making some much-needed cash."

"How?" I asked.

"We have been running drugs for Big Boy," Squeak said.

Honey screamed and said, "Squeak, you stupid bitch, you talk too damn much!"

Of course that weak bitch Squeak started crying, because that's all she ever does in a stressful situation. "Squeak, don't cry," said Tiny. Then she looked over at Honey and said, "So what if she told us? Remember your number one rule: no secrets." Honey couldn't say anything, so she just sucked her teeth and looked away. My thoughts traveled back in time, to when we decided to join forces and become a crew. We all made up a rule which we were all supposed to live by.

Honey's rule was no secrets. Squeak's rule was never to lie. Tiny's rule was we stand by each other, no matter what. Candy's rule was we get money by any means necessary, and my rule was never mess with someone who your crewmembers dealt with first. I thought we all lived by those rules until now. Candy's voice brought me back to reality, and what she was saying shocked me.

Candy said that she was going to kill Eddie, and then she asked us if we had her back.

Everyone told her yes at once. I said, "But we don't know where Eddie is."

Honey shocked us all by saying, "Don't worry about that, I already put the word out. I have eyes all over Harlem, and if Eddie is still around, we will know about it." Candy asked where was she going to stay, because the hospital was releasing her the next day. I told her not to worry about that. I had it covered.

I had moved all of her stuff to my house, and she would sleep in Karen's old bedroom. As I said the last word Honey said, "Te, I knew I had something to tell you. Karen is out there smoking crack, and Tommy and his brother are selling her ass all over town."

I yelled out, "What? Are you sure?"

"Yes I'm sure. Me and Squeak saw her ourselves yesterday. When we tried to talk to her about coming home, Tommy pulled her by her hair and told her she could only talk to customers and only when him and Johnny said so."

Then Candy surprised me again when she looked over at me and said that we would handle everything when she came home from the hospital. For the rest of the visit I was quiet. I couldn't even think straight. When visiting hours were over I could not wait to get home to call Danny's cell phone and let him know about Karen. I called him until I fell asleep. I was so drained I could not even write that night. I just knew something was wrong with Danny though, because he always answered his phone.

I was not sure what to do about anything in my life, hopefully the next few hours would bring me peace of mind and a whole lot of answers. The next day when I arrived at the hospital to pick Candy up, she was already dressed and ready to go. She signed her discharge papers, and we got out of there. When we reached the apartment, the rest of our crew was already there waiting for us. Candy went to her new room to put her things away and Honey went to the kitchen to make us something to eat. The rest of us went into the living room to watch some television, and just relax.

When the food was done everyone ate, and then Candy told us her plan. We were going to take back everything that was taken from us, and she meant everything. Candy would avenge her mother's murder, and we were going to get Karen off the street. And get her away from those pimping bastards who were trying to ruin her life. Tiny asked where would we start, and Candy said at the beginning.

First we needed money, and that's where Honey and Squeak came in. We would put the money we all had together and get some drugs from Big

Boy and start selling our own shit. The plan sounded real good, but would it be that easy? Candy said it wouldn't be, but we would do it anyway. Then she looked at Honey and asked her if she heard anything about Eddie,

Honey looked real happy all of a sudden. She said, "I almost forgot, I got the call twenty minutes before you came in! Big Boy's lieutenant, Hammer, said Eddie is staying on 112th Street, between Saint Nicholas and Seventh Avenue at that fleabag hotel. You know the one I'm talking about, the Ebony."

"Word, has he been there since all of this happened?" I asked.

"Yes," said Honey, "And Eddie is smoking crack and he is on it heavy." When I looked over at Candy I saw the wheels already turning and just like that, I saw that Candy knew how we would kill Eddie. We would give him some bad drugs, but first we had to see how much money we all had together. I had over three thousand dollars. That was money that Danny had been giving me that I'd been saving for a rainy day. And Candy had five hundred dollars, money that her mother gave her the night that she died.

She said, "That's why Eddie was beating her mother, because Mom would not give him any money." Now we know why he wanted it so bad, to buy crack. Honey and Squeak had six thousand between the both of them, and Tiny had five hundred dollars. She got it for her birthday, but was saving it for a rainy day also. So between the five of us we had ten thousand dollars, and the plan was set in motion.

Honey and Squeak left a little while later, and took five thousand with them to get the drugs. We were not sure if that was enough, but Honey said not to worry. She would handle everything, and we shouldn't sweat it. The next thing we had to do was take the GED test so we could be finished with this school shit and focus on what needed to be done. For the rest of the night the three of us just chilled, and watched television until sleep overcame us.

The next morning we were woken by a ringing telephone. When I answered the phone it was Squeak telling us to get ready. They would be here in an hour so we better be up. When we hung up I jumped in the shower and then Candy and Tiny got in. By the time that Honey and Squeak arrived we were ready to roll. First we stopped for breakfast at McDonalds, and then we went to the state building to register for the GED test.

The next test date was in two days, and they had room for all of us. With that taken care of Honey suggested that we go by her house so she could show us what they got from Big Boy the night before. When we got there the only one who was home was Honey's gay brother Dwayne, aka Sunshine, and his friend Donny, aka Rain. They were a hot mess and funny as hell. We knew we were in for some laughs, and as soon as the door closed behind us the jokes started.

Rain said, "Oh no Miss Thing," while looking straight at Tiny. "Where did you get those jeans from, and where can I go to buy some ass like that? Girl, your ass looks like it was molded by big brother bootie himself."

I had to ask, "Rain who is big brother bootie?"

He snapped his fingers, rolled his eyes, and said, "Who else? The butt fairy."

We all fell out laughing, and when I wiped the tears from my eyes I was looking straight at Candy, and once again I saw her wheels turning. She told the Queens, as they called their crew, that we would be right back. When we got in Honey's room she looked at all of us one at a time, then said, "I want the Queens down with our plan. What do you think?" I looked around at everyone's face and I knew that the deal was sealed.

Not a word was spoken as we headed back to the living room, and when we got there Candy explained to the Queens what we were doing. They called the rest of the Queens over for an emergency meeting. A half hour later Goldie, Swan, and Milkshake came gliding in, giving air kisses all throughout the room. After the hellos were done, Sunshine snapped her fingers, and called a private meeting. When they came back out they had a handful of money, which added up to five thousand dollars.

We would pool their money with our money, and we would all get money, and with determination in our eyes we were ready. We bagged up all the drugs What we bought would bring us back about fifteen thousand dollars. Then the next time we would just buy more to flip. We decided we would work in pairs—one Crimee paired with one Queen. We would stamp our bags with a butterfly so everyone would know our work from everyone else's.

We started in the West Village, and worked our way uptown. In one week's time all the drugs were sold, and we brought in twelve thousand dollars. We knew it would only get better from here, and we were ready for whatever came our way. With our GED test out of the way we could move on to step two, which was saving Karen from herself, and killing Eddie, whichever happened first. I still had not heard from Danny, and I was worried.

Even before I found out that Karen was caught up in the streets, I was worried about Danny. I did not want to involve the police just yet, because I did not know what Danny was involved in. I assumed he was selling drugs, but I wasn't really sure, so my girls and I would have to investigate that as well. My life was like a never-ending story, and in these last few weeks I didn't have any time to write my thoughts down. But soon I would have to take a breath, and put my thoughts down on paper to cleanse and purify my soul.

Chapter Four

Searching

I don't know where to begin
I don't know where it will end
I'm sitting outside
In a passing wind

My mind is filled with words
But I don't know how to lay them down
Every day I look outside my window
With my eyes always facing the cold hard ground

Because I'm really unhappy living this way
The problems never seem to go away
I'm always looking for a great escape
Trying to take away the never-ending pain

The shame, the anger, the hurt
All of these things I need to let go
Because if I don't release them soon
Inside I feel like I will explode

When the anger erupts
I know someone will get hurt
Because the pain is too much to bear
And there's no one around to trust

Wanting to run
To go to a far away land
Where I'll be so free
And I will let my feelings evaporate like dry sand

This poem was written at a time in my life when I was feeling very overwhelmed. I knew something was amiss, and very soon shit was going to blow up in my face. I just hoped that everyone in my circle would come out standing tall, instead of being six feet under ground.

My crew and I had a look out at the hotel where Eddie was staying. It was a cousin of Rain's, a guy who would sell his eighty-year-old mother for some money and drugs.

Buster had a room two doors down from Eddie, and he had been staying in the hotel for about a week now. Buster had befriended Eddie like we told him to do, and he was supplying him with drugs we were giving him to keep him high until we were ready to attack. We planned it for the next day—Friday the thirteenth. It was a day when evil lurked around every corner, and we were on the prowl. Word on the street was that Tommy, Johnny, and Karen had taken their business on the road. But with our business growing the way it was we had friends everywhere, and somebody was bound to run across them and send the word back up top to us. Until then we would lay low, after we performed the hit on this murdering bastard.

We all felt real good about what was about to go down. Revenge is so sweet. We would strike at 2:00 AM, and we would hit hard. As time passed we had stepped our game up. We still dealt with crack but we were also dealing weed and dope. Buster had gotten Eddie hooked on that brown horse. Since our shit was so good and quantity was never a problem, we kept Buster heavily supplied. A fiend was always going to be around for free drugs, so we had Eddie right where we wanted his dumb ass. This day we sent two Queens— Milkshake and Swan—to handle our distribution on the block.

Swan had already rented a room in the hotel so his face was already familiar around there. All the addicts would come to them, plus their friends who knew our stamp. We wanted to sell as much as we could, since this would be our last night in the Ebony. After tonight the block would be too hot. The plan was that at 1:30 AM Buster would tell Eddie that he had run out of drugs and he would go and cop some more. He would tell Eddie to give him a half hour and then he would be back. He told him not to open the door until he heard the signal.

It was 2 AM and it was showtime. Buster knocked on our hotel room door, two taps, and we knew it was on and popping. We had already relocated Buster; tomorrow he would be going to a drug treatment center downtown. He said it was time for him to take his life back, but for the night he said he was going to hang out with his brother Roland, aka Dope. Dope was a known stick up kid, who hung out at Seventy-one West 112th Street and Lenox Avenue. Roland told Buster his friends were giving a "get high" party. All you had to bring were a couple of bags of your choice to share, and you were in there like swimwear. It was on and popping for the junkies.

We gave Buster one thousand dollars in cash and five bags of dope. Buster thanked us and he was out like a flash of light. He said that if this was his last night getting high he was going out with a bang. We wouldn't know until the next day how right Buster was.

With Buster out of the way we split up. One Queen and one Crimee would be parked in the block in two different trucks for our escape routes.

We stationed two people everywhere—on the corner, the stoop, and cleaning out the hotel room, and then there was me and Candy. We walked up to room thirteen and tapped on the door three times. Eddie opened up the door to a chrome .380 nickel-plated handgun with a silencer pointed right at his fucking head.

Candy said, "What's up Eddie, remember me?"

Eddie stuttered, "Hey Candy, how have you and your mom been?" I saw a tear form in Candy's eye, and without another word we pushed into the room. Of course we had gloves on, but we still didn't want to touch anything. We made Eddie sit on the bed, and I pulled out the syringe filled with some uncut heroin and threw it at Eddie. He started stuttering again, "What do ya'll want me to do with that?"

Candy said, "Here's the deal, either you stick yourself or I will empty my whole clip in your ass. Now choose, motherfucker."

Eddie started crying, "Girl why are you doing this to me? Wasn't I always good to you and your mama?"

Her voice just a whisper, and with tears rolling down her face, she relived that unforgettable night. Candy told Eddie everything she remembered about that night. Then she looked up at him and said, "You took away the only somebody who ever loved me. Now I have nothing, and neither will you. I came here to watch you suffer and goddammit that's what I'm going to see. Now nigger—stick yourself!"

He picked up the needle and asked what was in it. Candy shot him in his right kneecap, and then in his left one, then she asked him if he had any more questions. Addicts are so dumb, so of course he asked another one.

"Candy if you knew where I was all this time, why didn't you turn me in to the cops?"

She looked at him and cracked a smile. She said, "Because they weren't going to kill you, and I wanted you dead like my mother." Then she shot him in his stomach and yelled, "Now bastard, stick yourself!" I turned the television up real loud just to cover up the screaming, because I could see that Candy was getting hysterical. But shit that was her mother, and I knew her pain. I guess the pain was becoming too unbearable for him, because Eddie picked up the needle and stuck it into his arm, hard.

He looked over and asked if we were we happy. Candy said, "Not quite," then she shot him in his dick. There was so much blood it was making me feel weak, but the job was almost done and in a few more minutes we would be gone. I could see the effects of the drugs; it was starting to take control over him. Eddie was shaking, kicking, and foaming at the mouth. It was really a disgusting sight.

When I looked over at Candy I caught a sudden chill. She was rubbing the gun and she had a sinister smile on her face. It was a smile of a stone-cold killer, and two seconds later it was over. Maria Ramos could finally rest in peace. Her killer was dead.

Chapter Five

It was 3:00 AM when we walked out of the Ebony and into the wind. Once we all reached my house the party began. We drank Hennessy and smoked purple haze until our eyes couldn't stay open any longer. The next morning Rain woke us all up with her screaming and crying. I went into the living room, and before I could ask what was wrong, the news anchor answered my question.

At Seventy-one West 112th Street, at approximately 5:00 AM, several bodies were discovered on the roof tied together and shot, execution style. There seemed to be no witnesses, and all the police had to go on was an anonymous phone call telling them to investigate this location. In an unrelated story there was a killing at the Ebony on 112th Street last night. At approximately 3:00 AM an unidentified Hispanic male was shot several times in one of the hotel rooms. Once again there were no witnesses in this case. The police were asking if anyone had any information on either of these crimes to call their tip line.

We were all sitting there in stunned silence, everyone left with their own thoughts until Rain said, "I know those were my cousins on the roof, and I'm going to find out what the hell went on in that building." Then she looked us all in our faces, and asked if we were with her. Of course the answer was yes, so it was on and popping once again.

Several days passed, and finally Rain's family was notified. They were going to cremate their bodies and sprinkle their ashes all over Harlem. When Squeak asked why, Rain said because Buster had gotten high all over Harlem. And Dope had stuck up every block from east to west, so it was only right. After all those arrangements were made we hit the streets to find out what happened in building 71 on that horrible night that took their lives.

When we hit the block we asked some cats who were in front of the building if they heard what happened that night. Of course they wanted to know what was in it for them. So Tiny pulled out two hundred dollar bills, and asked if this was enough. Of course it was. This tall slinky nigger named Rock started talking first.

He said, "Some dudes from Jefferson Houses had beef with Dope. He had robbed them last weekend, and they wanted revenge." Then he also told us about some other dudes from East River Houses. They also wanted Dope dead because he had been robbing them ever since he came home from jail. Dope had these cats so scared they were ready to close up shop, until they heard Dope was going to be in the building at the fiend extravaganza. All this information sounded good but we still didn't know who did the hit.

So I said, "Okay, Rock, all of that sounds good, but who pulled the trigger?"

Rock said, "Hold on pretty lady, I'm getting to that. A dude named Lucky killed them." He looked away.

"Who the hell is Lucky?" asked Goldie.

I looked over at Candy, and once again I saw her wheels turning. "Lucky, from 101st Street and Broadway."

"Exactly," replied Rock.

Candy turned to Tiny and said, "Give him the money." Then she snapped her fingers and we were out.

We were all starving so we decided to walk over to PD'S Steak House on 110th and Third Avenue. We were going to sit down, grab something to eat, and discuss the next phase of our plan.

Once we all had our food and were well into our meals, Swan turned to Candy and asked, "Who the hell is Lucky?" All eyes were on homegirl.

Candy looked at me and she said, "We went to school with Lucky, aka Lance Sullivan."

Then it sank in. Lance was a guy who wanted to get with Candy from the time he was able to speak.

"I thought he was locked up doing twenty to life for a double murder," I said.

"Well diva," Milkshake said, "I guess you thought wrong, now how do we find this fucking bastard?"

With that question in mind we all finished our meal, and headed back to my place. On the way there we bumped into Nakia and Shannon, two chicks we were cool with from Foster projects. They told us about a party that night on 103rd and Broadway at a little spot called Escape. It was a new club and it was always jumping. They said everybody and their mama was going to be there, so of course we would be there too. So we thanked them, and told them we would see them later on that night.

"This is perfect," said Squeak. "Hopefully that cat Lucky will be in there, because I am ready to get rid of his clown ass."

I felt the same way, but knew it was going to take a miracle to get him alone. I was hoping that he still had a thing for Candy, and if he did, we would use that to our advantage. All the Crimeez were going to my house to get ready for the party, while the Queens were going to Swan's house to do the same thing. There was a party in the village that they were going to breeze into, and they were taking some drugs to sell. Goldie said you could always find someone who wanted drugs in the village, and they were going to get that money. We air-kissed goodbye, and said that we would meet back up the next evening.

Chapter Six

When we arrived at Escape that night the party was already in full swing, and it was crowded as hell. You know all eyes were on us because we were dressed to kill, and we loved the attention. Squeak and Honey headed straight to the bar to grab a Henny and Coke on the rocks, while the rest of us went to find a booth and scope out the scenery. We were looking for Lucky, and just like I thought, he was right there in the mix of things. When our girls finally came over to the table, we hit the dance floor to get our party started.

I asked Candy what the plan was, and she said she was just going to play it by ear. That's when Lucky spotted her ass, and it was on from there. We partied well into the morning, and at 4:00 AM Lucky suggested that we go and grab a bite to eat.

We all said sure, but Candy said, "Why spend all that money when we could just go to Lucky's house and cook?"

I don't know if it was all the liquor or what, but Lucky's guard was down. He said okay, so we went to the bodega on his block and grabbed a few things. Then we went upstairs to his apartment. When we got inside, Candy gave me the bag.

She whispered, "Don't touch anything," and she took Lucky into the back. I don't know what happened back there, but twenty minutes later, Candy came out and told us it was time to bounce. Then she opened the door and we walked into the wind.

The next morning I called Swan's house and told them to come over for a meeting. When the Queens arrived you could tell they had some news to share with us, but that would have to wait. After the air kisses were out of the way, Candy told us what took place in that back room. She told us she undressed Lucky, put a condom on his dick, and rode him to Neverland. When he screamed out he was coming, she stuck him with the heroin-filled needle. Then she looked at Rain and said, "Your cousin's killer is dead."

All we heard was Rain sobbing, and Goldie telling him it would be okay. When Rain pulled himself together he told us their big news.

The night before, in the village, they ran into Chocolate, a drag queen they knew from the club. She told them about a show she went to see in Atlantic City. Then she asked if we still wanted information on that girl named Karen, with twin brothers as her pimps.

Goldie said, "I told her yes, and she said, 'Girl, those niggers got her strung out, and it wasn't a pretty sight.' Chocolate said if we were going to get her, we better move fast. They are thinking about taking their show on the road, to North Carolina."

I was angry, but before I could say a word, Candy asked me what time I wanted to leave. An hour later the Crimeez were on the road, and by mid-afternoon we were checking into Bally's hotel in Atlantic City.

We used Tiny's nickname, Monica Swawasky, to check in. It was a private joke amongst us, because Tiny loved to suck dick. We thought it was funny, but the desk clerk did not. He was very rude, but I found his attitude amusing. He was just mad that nobody wanted him to suck their dick. We took our bags upstairs, and then we hit the casino to spend some of this drug money we had made. The whole day all we did was drink and gamble. Then at 7:00 PM some guys handed us a flyer with my sister's picture on it.

Karen was butt-naked with a dick in her mouth, and a Spanish chick with a strap-on was fucking her in her ass from the back. No more was Karen the sweet-faced girl who wanted to become a doctor. Now she was known as Pearl, a well-known porno starlet. I was totally disgusted, and those pimping bastards were going to pay real fucking soon. We still had a few hours to play around with, but I lost my edge and told the girls I was going to the room to lie down. Squeak and Honey said they were going to check out the other casinos, so that left Candy and Tiny on their own.

They said they would be upstairs by 11:30 PM so we could come up with a plan. By 11:45 the plan was set. Candy had found some masks to cover our faces and by 12:05 we were knocking on the hotel room door. We paid our twenty dollar entrance fee, and we were in there like swimwear. We didn't see Karen at first, but there were two other chicks performing oral sex on each other. The show was disgusting but Squeak and Honey were all into it. I wondered what that was all about, but this wasn't the time to question it.

About an hour later they finally introduced Pearl. When Karen came out she was wearing a red see-through crotch-less teddy. She looked stoned out of her mind. She was moving like a zombie—real robot-like and shit. I had to restrain myself from snatching her ass up off the goddamn floor. This bitch was doing anything and everything, and it was so fucking degrading. All I could think was hopefully her show wouldn't last too much longer. After an hour of pure filth it was finally over.

We waited until all the guests were gone, then Tiny left to take our stuff from the room to the car. Honey took Karen to the bathroom and made her get dressed. Then she took her to wait for us downstairs. Now it was time for us to execute our plan. Squeak was going to clean the living room and wipe down everything to remove any fingerprints. While Candy and I crept to the bedroom, like cats on the prowl, there was one thing on my mind. I had not seen the pimps since Karen's show first started. They were probably in the room counting her fucking money. Bastards, but they were about to be in for the shock of their useless lives.

Candy opened the door with the gun drawn, ready to blow a motherfucker's head off. And would you believe they were in there sniffing coke out of a straw, not even aware of their surroundings?

When they noticed that we were standing there, the darker one said, "Who the fuck are you?"

I said, "I'm Karen's sister."

"Who the fuck is Karen?"

Before I could say a word Candy shot both of them in their dicks.

They were screaming at the top of their lungs, so Candy said, "Te, stick these niggers so we can get the fuck out of here," and that's just what I did.

After I injected the light-skinned twin I turned to darkie and said, "You know my sister as Pearl." And just when recognition reached his eyes, he drew his last breath. We got down to the car fast and were on the highway in seconds. The ride home was quiet, and Karen slept for most of the way. But when she was up she was very agitated, and she kept asking where Tommy was.

I tried to ignore her dumb ass but it was becoming hard. Homegirl was really trying my patience. Thank God we were crossing the city limits as I was having these thoughts. When we reached our house I told Karen to go into the bathroom and take a nice long bath. Honey went to the kitchen to make us something to eat. We had steak with red potatoes and white rice. After that meal we were all exhausted, so we called it a night. Even though it was already the next morning, I called the Queens. Goldie picked up. I told him we were home, and everything had gone well. We talked for a minute longer, and then I told Goldie we would get together with them tomorrow. Then I climbed in the bed.

Chapter Seven

The next day someone was banging on my apartment door like they were the police. Then I thought, *What if it is the police, all the shit that we were into it would be just our luck.* And don't you know when I looked through the peephole, I almost messed my pants. Sure enough it was two suits, one black and one Hispanic, so I said a prayer and opened the door.

The Hispanic officer said, "Good afternoon, my name is Detective Lopez, and this is my partner, Detective Murphy. Are you Tasha Heart?"

I was scared, but I replied, "Yes, I am Tasha Heart. Is there a problem officers?" "Yes there is. May we come in for a minute?"

I stepped aside. When they were seated the detective said, "We are sorry to inform you but your brother, Daniel Heart, is dead."

I took a deep breath, exhaled, and then I asked them to tell me what happened to my brother. They told me he was found on 155th Street and Eighth Avenue cut up in a dumpster. He was found over a week ago, but his prints did not come back until that morning.

"We are very sorry for your loss, but we need for you to come down and identity his body." That's all that I remembered until I opened my eyes a little while later.

I woke up in my bed with my girls gathered around me. I looked each one of them in their face, and then I asked them what happened. With tears in her eyes Honey told me what I already knew in my heart. I had fainted and my only brother was dead. She told me everything the detective said, and then she said that I blacked out for about forty-five minutes. Tiny had already gone to view Danny's body, she pretended to be Karen. She said that there could be no funeral for Danny because he was cut up into too many pieces. So I would have him cremated, and put his ashes on the living room wall unit.

The pain I was feeling was truly unbearable. I just wanted to block everything out, but I couldn't. Then I looked around for Karen, and she wasn't there. I looked straight at Candy, and she said, "Baby, Karen is gone.

She couldn't handle the news about Danny, and she ran out the house right after you collapsed. When Tiny and Squeak went after her, she was already in the wind."

All I could do was cry. I cried for my family, I cried for all the drama in my life, and I also cried because I knew the police would be bringing me some more bad news real soon.

One week passed with no word on who killed Danny. Karen's whereabouts were still a mystery also. Then one day the detectives were back, knocking on my apartment door again, just like I thought they would. This time they came to tell me that my sister had overdosed off of some bad heroin in an abandoned building. There was nothing left for me to say. Now I would be cremating my older sister as well as my older brother.

Then Detective Murphy smiled and said, "We are very sorry about your sister, but we do have some news on your brother's murder. We got an anonymous tip, and we are looking at a suspect as we speak." Then he told me that when they knew something, they would notify me."

The only good news I got was our GED results came that day and not surprisingly we all passed with flying colors. But how could I be happy about that when my life was falling apart. Two days later I had my brother, Danny, and my sister, Karen, cremated, I could not stand to attend another funeral. So I celebrated the only way I knew how, by staying drunk and high for my family members who were no longer here.

My girls cleaned out Danny's bedroom, and under his bed were some of his old notebooks, which shed some light on what he was into and who may have killed him. It seemed that Danny controlled the drug game from 152nd Street to 155th Street. He was selling coke, weed, and dope, and he was making a killing. He had become romantically involved with a twenty-year-old woman named Shyann Johnson. She was from the Polo Grounds projects, around the same area where Danny was killed.

The relationship started last December, and from the letters they both wrote you could tell that they were really feeling each other. All was going good until the previous month. Shyann wrote that she had a crazy ex-boyfriend named Pop. He had just come home from jail, and apparently he would not take no for an answer. He told Shyann that if he ever saw Danny up there again he would kill him. All I was thinking was that this was a lot of information from an unexpected place.

My girls told me not to worry about anything, they said they would get all the information we would need to take care of this new problem. Thank God for my friends, because I could not cope with day-to-day living. I couldn't write, I wasn't eating or sleeping, and I didn't even bathe. All I did was lie in my bed and stare at the ceiling, wanting this nightmare to end.

Squeak and Honey went to see Big Boy to get some information on
this Pop character, and of course Big Boy knew the score. First he told
them that Pop had just come home from doing an eight-year bid in jail for
murder. Pop wanted Danny's blocks because he saw how much bread he
was making, and he wanted it all. He felt this was his block, so why should
he let another nigger from somewhere else come and take something from
him that he felt he deserved? Even though he'd been gone for eight years,
none of that mattered. When he heard Danny was fucking with Shyann it
was on and popping from there."

Then he said, "Pop goes to Mr. Nix's gambling spot on 152nd Street
and Eighth Avenue every night at ten o'clock sharp. He stays inside until
his money runs out, which is usually around 3:00 AM." With that piece of
news Squeak and Honey called the Queens and told them to get over to
my house fast. Then they headed back to my place. When they arrived the
Queens had just walked in, so Candy called the meeting to order. Honey
then took the floor, and told us what Big Boy had said.

Then she asked, "How do we proceed?"

That's when Rain spoke up. He said that the Queens would handle this
hit since we took care of Lucky for him. With that out of the way, Goldie
snapped his fingers, and said he had the perfect idea. They would do the
hit dressed as men. Swan looked over at him and said, "Now that's sweet."
Goldie continued on with the plan. That night Sunshine, Milkshake, and
Goldie would get to the spot around 11:00 PM. They would mingle with the
crowd inside, while Rain and Swan were parked outside for the getaway.

When Pop walked out of the spot that next morning, he would have a
big surprise waiting for his ass. For the rest of the evening I could not do
anything. All I did was think. I was hoping everything would go well, and
I could not wait for all the drama to end. At 4:00 AM the telephone rang,
and when I answered all I heard was, "P-o-p is now d-o-a. All I thought
was, *Thank God, shit now maybe I can get some much-needed sleep.*

Chapter Eight

Since the execution of Pop, shit was real quiet, and I was still in mourning, doing much of nothing on a day-to-day basis.

One night Candy, Tiny, and I were playing the card game pity pat. Out of nowhere Tiny said, "Squeak and Honey are fucking each other."

I looked over at her and said, "Could you repeat yourself?"

But before she could say anything else, Candy said, "I already knew that." Now I really looked around at them all crazy.

I looked up at the ceiling, and said out loud, "I guess everyone knew but me." I made jokes, trying to lighten the mood, but when I caught my reflection in the mirror it frightened me. I looked real bad. It looked like I had lost twenty to thirty pounds, and my hair and nails were a mess. So I decided to change that right away. First I took a hot shower, washed my hair, and then I oiled my body down.

I put on my silk pajamas, changed my bed sheets, and then I looked in the mirror and told myself tomorrow would be a new day. Then I went back into the living room, sat down, and said, "Tell me everything I missed in the last few weeks." Tiny told me that she believed that Squeak and Honey's love affair had started months ago, and they acted like they were really in love.

"How did you find out about it," I asked.

She said, "I walked in on them kissing one day."

"Well, what did they do?"

"They didn't do anything," Tiny said, "They just acted like everything was normal. You know how nasty Honey is. Well, she looked me in my face and said, 'Now you know. We're lovers and have been for a while, and we don't care what any of you say about it.'"

I was staring at Tiny with my mouth hanging open, then I looked at Candy and said, "Now tell me how you know."

"It's obvious. They were real secretive, always touching, and sneaking around so one day I asked them."

"What did they say?"

Candy looked at me and said, "You know how that punk bitch Squeak is, all she did was put her fucking head down. But that evil bitch Honey rolled her eyes at me and told Squeak to lift her head up, and then she told her she had nothing to be ashamed of. Then she looked at me, rolled her eyes again like I was interrupting something, and then she said, 'Look, we have been an item since January, and we didn't know how to tell you guys. That's why we kept it a secret for so long.' Then she asked me was I going to tell the rest of the crew. I said no, if you want them to know you should tell them yourself."

"Well, I guess they didn't want me to know," I said.

All was quiet and then Tiny dropped another bombshell on us. She said she was three months pregnant by the Spanish kid from her building and they were getting married in two weeks. Congratulations were in order and then Candy asked her why she didn't tell us.

Tiny said, "So much was going on, the time just wasn't right." At that point the doorbell rang. It was Swan and Sunshine and they were hysterical.

Sunshine said, "Goldie and Milkshake were just in a car accident on 127th Street, and they are both dead."

I asked, "Where is Rain?"

"Rain's disappeared," Swan said, "He has been missing since a week ago, and the police suspect foul play but there is still no body." I held Swan while Tiny held Sunshine, and we all just cried together. Some time had passed and then Candy went to the liquor store for a couple of bottle of Hennessy to dull our never-ending pain. After five hours of crying, and after three thirty-dollar bottles of Hennessy, we were beyond drunk. But at least we had stopped crying. Everyone was lost in their own thoughts

Everyone was just mellow, and withdrawn into themselves. Not knowing what else to do we all went to bed to dry out and get ready for another disaster of a day. We stayed in the house twisted out of our minds until the day of Goldie and Milkshake's funerals. They would be held together because their families knew how close they were and it was only fitting. The day of their home-going service the skies opened up, and the heavens rained heavily for our fallen Queen's. It was a sad day. Swan, and Sunshine were not handling it well at all.

After the burial of Michael Anthony King, known to the world as Milkshake, and Garrett Davon Jones, known as Goldie, we went straight to my house and started drinking all over again. We were drunk forever it seemed like, and we didn't stop until we finally received some news on Rain's disappearance. Two weeks after the funeral, Sunshine got a call from

Donny's mother. She told him that Rain's body was just found in a hallway staircase in the Polo Grounds. Coincidence—we thought not. So now someone else was going to die.

There would be no funeral for our fallen friend because just like Danny, Rain was cut up real bad, and whoever killed him had held his dead body for days so it was badly decomposed when he was found. He was cut up and thrown out like a bag of fucking garbage. He did not deserve to die like that, so we got drunk for another fallen Queen. May God rest his soul, Donny Theodore Evans, may he rest in peace. Death just seemed to follow us everywhere we went, and before we could find out who killed Rain we got some more devastating news.

The news report went as followed. In a fit of rage, an eighteen-year-old female named Sara Bell had just shot and killed her seventeen-year-old lover Heather Graham, and then killed herself. I could not believe this shit. That news anchor was talking was about Honey and Squeak, and did she say they were dead? From what we could gather Squeak wanted out of their relationship, and Honey was not having it. So in a moment of fury Honey snapped and they were both dead with gunshot wounds to the head.

Immediately I picked up the phone and called Honey's house and spoke to her mother, Mrs. Bell. After we heard the news on television about his sister's death, Sunshine was in no condition to speak to his family or anyone else for that matter. He was numb. In a short period of time he had lost his sister by blood and his sisters in sprit. Shit was real fucked up, and when his mother answered I expressed my sympathy for her loss. She told me there would be no funeral for my friend, they were going to have her cremated because she was shot with a nine millimeter in her left eye and half of her face was blown off.

She asked me if I knew where Sunshine was at, and I told her he was right here hurting, but I said we would take care of him. She said something else, but all I remember was saying goodbye and then I just stared off into space. After that conversation I was numb, and just started crying for my friends, their families, and me. Ten minutes later I walked in the living room and told my crew what I just heard, and once again the drinking started.

Candy called Squeak's mom to give our condolences and to find out about her funeral arrangements. Mrs. Graham said she was taking her baby back to Baltimore tomorrow, and she would be buried next to her father. Then she asked if we knew that the two girls were a couple. Candy could not tell her the truth—it would break her heart, because she was really into church and raised her daughter as a devout Christian.

So she told a lie and said no, we had no idea that they were involved with each other. The conversation ended there, and it was all for the best because Candy was too drunk too keep on talking. We needed to put a plan together fast, so Tiny went to see Big Boy to find out if he had heard anything about Rain's death. And just like we thought, he knew everything that had taken place. He told Tiny that one of his workers was there the day that Honey and Squeak came by asking questions about Pop. That same dude was Shyann's older brother, Shawn. Shawn was Pop's right hand man, so once Pop turned up dead his crew knew who did it, and they plotted to kill our whole crew. They just happened to catch that faggot nigger first, and that was all she wrote.

Chapter Nine

When Tiny came home and relayed her conversation with Big Boy to us we were all heated. But the remaining Queens were ready to start a fucking war, so we sat down and plotted. Big Boy also told Tiny everything that we needed to know about Shyann and her brother Shawn. He gave us their address, where they hung out at, what church their mother went to, and what day she went grocery shopping. So once again it was on and popping.

The night finally arrived, October 31st. Yes Halloween, the day when we would avenge our fallen friend and family member. We picked that night because on Halloween night in Harlem there was always something going on, and we would blend right in with whatever we ran into. Sunshine went to the village and got our masks for us so we had a disguise. We would be going as the Cosby kids. I bet none of them would have ever done anything like what we were about to do.

It was finally 9:00 PM and time to roll. We were going to drive uptown, into the projects. When we got there, Tiny would stay by the car in her Theo mask with the engine running for our getaway. We would go to their house as the Huxtable sisters and handle our business quick; we would be in and out of there in less then twenty minutes. We walked to building number four with a little pep in our step. Shit, we were hyped up. You know that feeling you get, right before you kill someone? Well if you never killed anyone before, it's the same feeling you get right before you have a fight. It was exhilarating. You just feel untouchable and unstoppable, just like a super hero.

We took the steps up to the sixth floor, and soon we were standing in front of apartment 6F. The hallway was empty just the way we wanted it to be. Swan knocked on the door and said, "Trick or treat." All was quiet, and then we heard a loud boom and Swan's head was no longer attached to his body.

Then I heard a voice say, "You bitches thought you could sneak up on me, never! I'm fucking everywhere. I have eyes everywhere and now you're all dead."

I guess we all had the same thought—we all backed up toward the staircase. If we could just make it back to the car, we were good. But when I looked over my shoulder there was a guy holding a 45-caliber pistol, and he was pulling the trigger. Sunshine took one in the shoulder, but he wasn't going down without firing back. He got off two good shots, and homeboy was dead. He told us to run, and said he would cover us.

So we started running down the steps with our guns out front. We heard a door open and more shots were fired. I yelled for Sunshine, but he yelled back for us to keep going. He said he was right behind us, and then out of nowhere some dude was standing in our way. He had on a Freddie Krueger mask and a glove with knives on them. We didn't know if he was one of them or not, but it was our life or his. So Candy and I both fired and just kept on running.

It seemed to be taking us forever to get out of this building. Just one more flight, and we would be free. But when we got to the lobby Shyann had Tiny with a knife to her throat. When she saw us turn the corner, she slit her throat. Candy yelled, "No!" and emptied her clip into that bitch. And when she had no more bullets left, she went over to Shyann and started kicking and spitting on her. Candy was screaming so loud but no words were coming out of her mouth. It seemed like she was in a state of shock.

So I grabbed her by her coat and pulled her out of the building. We were immediately surrounded by more Halloween masks then I could count, and it seemed like every one of them had weapons. I pulled Candy back inside and grabbed Tiny and Shyann's guns, then I prepared myself to go all out. I slapped Candy to wake her up, and told her she had to pull herself together. Thank God the light was coming back into her eyes, and then she looked at me and said, "Let's do this."

At that same moment Shawn came around the corner, and saw his sister's dead body and he went berserk. I don't know why he didn't use the gun in his hands. Instead, he came rushing toward us, and before we could fire, Sunshine came around the corner like Rambo blasting. It didn't seem like the shots were fazing him because he was still coming at us, so we started shooting too. I have never seen someone take that many hits and stay standing.

Shawn was being lifted off his feet by the bullets, and he was still standing. Was *this nigger human, or what?* I asked myself. Candy took aim and hit Shawn dead in his forehead, and he came crashing down. We knew we couldn't go out the front of the building, so we made a beeline for the back exit. Surprisingly the back way was clear. Now all we had to do was make it to the car. It was twenty feet away, now ten. We were running scared, and Sunshine was bleeding real bad, and just when we reached the car we heard a loud blast. Sunshine went down hard, two shots to the back of the head, and we had to leave his dead body in the street. I didn't want to leave him but we were running for our lives, and there was nothing else that we could do.

Candy had the car door open, and I was still blasting my guns while getting into the car. Once I was inside Candy pulled off driving like a bat out of hell, and that's when I heard the police sirens on our ass. There was nowhere left for us to go, and nowhere for us to hide. Candy looked at me, and she told me that she loved me, and then she floored the gas. We were flying down 8th Avenue doing over eighty miles per hour when Candy lost control of the car.

There was nothing for us to do but pray, grab hands, and accept our fate. We hit the wall hard on 137th Street and Eighth Avenue, and we were pronounced dead at the scene. This was our tragic story, and now you know how it ended. Fucked up right? You wish that it didn't end this way right, well so do we.

Epilogue

I heard sounds, but couldn't place the words. I heard voices, but couldn't see the faces. Then I heard as clear as day, "She just moved her hand. Go and call the doctor."

I fought to open my eyes, and when I finally did I was in shock. My whole family was there: Mama, Danny, Karen, and even my home girls the Crimeez.

I could not believe this; I must be dead or on my way there. Out of nowhere I felt someone poking at me and calling my name.

I heard, "Tasha if you can hear me, blink your eyes."

I guess I did that because all I heard was, "Thank God, she's going to make it." Three days later I found out what had happened to me.

The day my mother had her car accident, I was with her. I had a doctor's appointment, and I met my mother at her job that day. On our way uptown we were in a three-car pileup, and I had been in a coma for the last six weeks. The doctors did not think that I would make it. But my mother never gave up hope, that's why I'm alive today. Two weeks after I came home from the hospital, I was ready to talk.

I told my family and friends everything that I thought had happened in my life while I was in the coma. Then I looked over at Honey and asked about her brother and his friends. She laughed, and said they were chilling, all of them were alive and doing well.

Then when I looked over at my mother she smiled at me, and then she laughed and said, "Baby girl, that was one crazy dream you had."

And all I could say was, "Yeah. it was A Crazy Harlem Dream."

Dreams

Sometimes dreams come in all shapes and sizes
They take you to places awake you will never go
They can be good and bad

True or false or a little in-between
Dreams take you to places
Places you never thought you would see

You're always wishing and hoping
With your eyes closed tight
Because when they are open
You are looking deep for love and acceptance

Making decisions for yourself
These decisions not always working out for the best
Always looking for a great escape
But never finding one awake

Looking for a higher power
We all have different names for them
Because not everyone calls them the same
But one thing we all have in common
We all dream for a lighter brighter day

On this green earth that we live on
Everyone has a dream and a goal
But in order for us to achieve it
We may travel different roads
But I always want you to remember

To never give up hope
Because throughout your many struggles and disap-
    pointments
Your dreams should always show you that you are
    tough
And if only for one day, minute, or second—that one
    wish you can touch

The End

Circles

A Novel

Prologue

This is the story of survival, my survival. Come along with me on this journey of life. See if I am strong enough to make it. Sleep has always been a problem for me, even when I was tired it would not come to me easily. When I finally close my eyes, I always see a bright light and hear a gentle voice whispering my name. I guess it's because my life has always been so dark.

When I am awake I wish for a miracle. I look for a knight in shining armor to save me from all this insanity that surrounds my life. I know that sometimes the direction in life that we travel leads us down different paths that can prevent us from doing the right thing. It is up to us to make it through and come out standing tall. Just remember, not all wishes come true.

Chapter One

A New Beginning

The year was 1994. The night was extremely hazy and hot, and let me tell you so was I. Now I know my fast ass was supposed to be in the house, doing absolutely nothing, just bored out of my fucking mind. Shit, I would probably be asleep at this very moment, but damn my tight non-virginal pussy was soaking wet, begging me to find a huge, hard cock to soak up all its juices. But first let me hip you to a few things about my world back then. Number one, dick was out there falling from the sky, and number two, with my looks and body, I could get any cock that I wanted, easy! And last but not least, number three. There were so many different circles of guys running around out there dying to have relations with us—that's me and my homegirl, Nina—that we could have dick for weeks to cum. In our world we were thrust into many different circles, whether it's guys we sleep with or friends that we hang out with, but not all of these circles were good for us.

Now before we get into all that, let me explain a little bit about myself. My name is Jazmine Marie Roberts, and I am a five-foot-five inches tall African-American albino female. I am the sexiest albino alive, and I call myself the blond bombshell. I have long blonde hair that touches my big round ass, and if you saw me in passing you would have swore that I was of a mixed breed or something. And if you felt the smooth texture of my hair it would seem as if I had a little bit of Indian in my family.

I have hazel eyes, which change from green, to brown, to gray, but they mostly change with my mood. I am beyond sexy, and yes all the hair on my body is blonde. My measurements are thirty-eight, twenty-six, thirty-six. Now imagine that, a black sister with a white, sexy body, and blonde all over. Shit, a man would have the best of both worlds fucking with me. Don't hate— now moving right along with the story.

I knew my lame ass sister was around here somewhere, watching my every fucking move, and when I ran into her ass it was going to be nothing but drama, because it always was with her. But I wasn't going home just yet! I flat out fucking refused, not until I found a HHC—that's a huge hard cock—to take away my sexual desires, and right then my young tender body needed its daily fix. Besides, my best friend Nina could stay out all night long if she felt like it, and she wasn't ready to send it in yet either.

My homegirl Nina is a banging Spanish butterfly. She stands five-foot-seven inches tall with a big black girl booty. Nina has thick, pretty bowlegs, a small waist, and breasts for days. She has a beautiful set of midnight blue eyes, something you do not see very often on a person of Hispanic descent. Her crazy mother, Wella, said that she got her eyes from her father, a man unknown to her. Nina had the sexiest bowlegged walk in history, and long, black, flowing hair that went way past her voluptuous behind.

Nina's motto was, why should she have to go upstairs early, when her mother Wella was probably out here looking for some dick to quench her thirst as well? Wella is the sexiest Spanish vixen I had ever known in my life. She is five-feet-eight inches tall, and she walks like one of those supermodels that you see on television. She always wears heels, and has her hair cut in a sexy style just like Halle Berry used to wear. She has an ass bigger and firmer then me and Nina put together, and all these other bitches out on the street too.

Homegirl was funny as hell too, plus she always told it like it was. On many nights she would say to us, "You little hot asses better stop fucking them niggers out there in the streets for free, and then you both come up in here hungry like yous ain't ate in days. Looking at me to cook a meal, like I'm fucking Betty Crocker or somebody. Shit, I want to be out in the street too!

"Shit, mamas, my motto is if you want to fuck this pussy, first you have to pay this bitch. Those motherfuckers never ask any questions either; they just put the money in my hands." Then she looked at us, cracked a smile, and walked off strutting her stuff.

It seemed to work every time too, motherfuckers don't play when it comes to Wella's pussy. Honey was the bomb; at least that's what motherfuckers around our way said. We lived in Saint Nicholas projects in Harlem. It had two sides, five buildings on one side and ten on the other. Wella knew all the men and even some of the women there, but nowhere else. She only went from 127th Street to 131st Street between Seventh and Eighth Avenue, but homegirl got her money so I was not mad at her.

Now a few days after Wella gave us her class—Whoring 101—I was standing in front of my building, chilling. Smoking a cigarette, minding my own damn business, and here comes my sister, Shonda, and her broke-ass boyfriend, Tyrone. I just knew some bullshit was about pop off, because that's what usually went down between us. Let me fill you in on Shonda's stink ass. She is five-foot-three inches tall, and dark-skinned with the flattest ass known to mankind. If you saw us together you would not believe for one second that we were related, let alone sisters.

She has long black hair that she always wears in a tired ponytail, and dark green eyes that match her complexion perfectly. She really wasn't bad looking but her attitude let you know she was a nasty bitch, and if you got to know her you wouldn't like her ass either. Shonda and Ty, as he called himself, have been together for five years, and they had a three-year-old son named Tyrone Junior. I love my sister and nephew very much but big Ty is a bitch-ass nigger and a liar and I could not stand his punk ass. But we will get to that later on in the story.

I walked over to them, and said, "Hey, Sis, what's up!"

But before she could open her mouth, Ty piped up with his broke ass, "Hi, Jazmine, you're looking real good today, shit what's going on with you?"

Then the bastard had the nerve to wink his eye at me like he was sexy or even fuckable for that matter, give me a fucking break. Now I was so fucking pissed off all I could do was close my eyes take a deep breath, and spit at his feet. If I said something to him for sure my sister would not be happy, and I would never do anything to hurt my blood, even though she gets on my damn nerves all the time. I did not understand how she could be so stupid and blind. Angry as all hell, I just turned away from them, and started to walk away to catch up with Nina. She was standing up the block at the corner store, talking.

I had only taken two steps when that bitch Shonda had the nerve to ask me some bullshit!

"Jazmine, what time is your grown-ass going upstairs?"

I looked back at her, and rolled my eyes real hard.

"In a little while," I said, and just kept on going, whispering under my breath, "Dumb bitch."

Shonda was twenty-two and I was seventeen. We had no parents so she was my legal guardian, and she had a little bit of authority, but not much. Anyway she needed to mind her own damn business, and worry about why her man was out here fucking the whole world from east to west. God, sometimes I really hate that bitch. I took three deep breaths trying to calm my nerves and I kept it moving.

When I got to the store, Nina was talking to two guys from our block named Mel and Ron who have been trying to fuck us for years. They were not bad looking, but they had two very big problems. They both had girlfriends, two big sisters named Michelle and Rochelle, who were twins. Those bitches were crazy as hell, so giving those niggers some pussy was out of the question, especially for free. Of course curiosity killed the cat, so I walked over anyway to see what was popping.

I said, "Fellas, what's good?"

Mel looked over at me and said, "You're what's good, Jazz," and cracked a killer smile which had me wet instantly!

Mel is tall, dark chocolate, and fine as hell. He has dimples that made you want to cum on yourself, but I heard his dick wasn't worth the trouble! The hood said he was short like a pickle and thin like a spaghetti noodle, now could you imagine some shit like that? But his money was extra long, so fuck it if shit ever went down between us I knew that I would be well-compensated for my time. Rochelle was on his back though, and in his pocket front and back. That big bitch walks around with blades in her hair, mouth, and in her bra, and she's built like an Amazon. Michelle is crazy too, but she's much quieter with her shit.

That scared me even more, because with someone like Michelle you never knew what they were thinking. Shit I've seen her in action, honey would just snap and you wouldn't even see it coming until it was way too late. In the end, it was never good for the person who felt her wrath. Ron was also a cutie, in his own way! Short, stocky, and light-skinned, and the streets said he was holding a nice-sized package but he did not know what to do with it. He always wanted the same position, straight missionary!

What female in their right mind, always wanted to be on the bottom? I guess after fucking that big-assed girl for so many years, Ron must have said fuck that shit! She is not getting on top and squashing me.

My thoughts were running wild, and a big smile appeared on my face. I had to laugh out loud. Then my ace in the hole, Nina, interrupts my thoughts, and pulled me to the side and whispers, "Jazz, let's slide with these cats tonight, you know we need the money! Wella is right, why should motherfuckers keep getting it for free when we're running around here broke, hungry, and wet? All we ever have at the end of the night is a dry pussy and empty pockets, but that shit will change tonight! They said they will give us five hundred dollars apiece, and they swear those twin towers will never find out about us."

I looked over at Mel. He was licking his tongue out at me, looking real tempting, plus I was beyond broke.

"Okay I'm with it," I said, "but they have to meet us someplace else because you know how the street talks." I started thinking, and then it came to me to tell them to meet us on 125th Street at the state building on Seventh Avenue and we would leave from there. Nina set it up, and twenty minutes later we were off to become working girls, no more fucking for free. We had a new beginning.

Once we met up with them, we went straight to a hotel in Trenton, New Jersey called the Hot Spot. It was very nice, not high class, but not one of those cheap, low budget ones either, and it would definitely serve its purpose for the night. We shared the same room and got busy as soon as the door closed. Clothes came off in a matter of seconds and I sucked Mel's dick like my life depended on it. Nina could perform with the best of them but I didn't think she was putting on an act, the way she was screaming out Ron's name and shit!

Ron must have been putting in overtime, but poor Mel, overtime could not help that thin twig that he called a penis! But I could have won an award for the way that I carried on! If anyone walked by our room all they heard was the bed squeaking, and loud moans of pleasure. Two hours and five hundred dollars later, Mel and Ron were out like a light.

When Nina saw that they were both asleep, she made up a little rap. Similar to what Lil' Kim said in her rap song a few years ago, we sucked them to sleep and went to get something good to eat. , Just kidding with you. Actually, we laid down until the morning, sweet dreams.

The next morning we split up at the same spot where we met them. Before we departed, they asked when could they see us again, and we told them whenever their money was right. Since they were holding major paper, we thought that would be sooner then later. But we never saw them again after that night, and we wondered why. We didn't have to wonder too long though, because you know how the streets are always talking, and in everybody's business

It wasn't too long before we found out what happened to them, and it was not good news either. Three weeks after we fucked them, Mel and Ron were shot and killed out in Brooklyn because of a drug deal gone bad. It took so long for them to be identified because the blast from the machine guns blew their faces to pieces. Since neither one of them had IDs on them, and since they had never been arrested in their lives, their prints weren't on file. After several days of not hearing from her son, Mel's mother filed a missing person's report, and her worst fears were confirmed a few days later. Her son and his longtime friend were dead.

Chapter Two

Getting Paid

Nina and I were far from virgins when we fucked Mel and Ron, but in a way we were virgins to the whoring game. Nina had lost her virginity at the age of thirteen to a kid from our building named Dee. And I lost my virginity at the tender age of twelve, to this grown man named John from around our way. But this was the first time we got paid for giving it up, and we discovered that we liked sex better with money. Getting paid felt real good, and we swore that we would never be broke again. We felt that we had no other skills to make money in the outside world, so we really had no other choice but to sell our bodies, and it paid very well.

Since Wella was always about the money whenever she got some dick, it seemed only natural for us to follow in her footsteps and become women of the night just like her. It just took us only a second to put our game face on, sit back, watch, and learn the ropes from the number one prostitute out there. Shit, Wella was her own pimp, and she was a natural-born hustler, so how could we go wrong? Money makes the world go round, and ours was going around in circles.

One night out of the blue, Wella said, "I know you little hussies are out there getting paid for giving up that young pussy yous got." She was looking us dead in our faces and then she gave out a little laugh, and told us that she was proud of us before she turned her head away. When she looked back our way again she said, "I hear stories about your little sexcapades out there. And it's all good with me as long as you remember the number one rule: get that money." Then she laughed again, and said, "Cause mamas, you know yous did learn from the best. But check this here, mamas. Wella is fucked up in the game right now, and I need to hold four hundred dollars for the bills this month."

Now all I'm thinking is either Wella's pussy is dried out, or nigger's money is real short. Either way, Wella was my girl and I loved her. Besides between Nina, and myself we had ten thousand dollars saved up from all the sexcapades that we were having, so four hundred dollars was nothing to us, it was small change to money-getters like us. Also Wella had been sick for the past four months, and we didn't know what was wrong with her so anything she wanted she could get.

She had gone to the doctor two days earlier for a complete checkup, but her results were not back yet. The doctor said it would take about a week before we knew anything, so all we could do was wait. I felt really sad. Wella was the only mother I had since my real mother was dead. She was shot down like a dog in the fucking street on her way home from work by her perverted-ass boyfriend, Sammy. Sammy raped me for four straight years, any chance he got. Over and over again, and it seemed like nothing was ever going to make him stop.

I was sad when he shot and killed my mother, but I was overjoyed when the police killed him. Sammy would not surrender when the cops told him to drop his gun, so they opened fire on him. He was hit fifteen times all over his body, and he died on the scene. I just wish it could have happened differently, leaving my mother still alive and in my life. But hey that's life, and sometimes you never get what you wish for.

Nina and I went out on dates six days a week, and we were having a ball in our new life, but we took one day for a rest day. Sunday was the Lord's day, and before Wella got sick she would say all good working women closed up shop for God on that day. Wella went to church every Sunday, so of course we went with her. She said the Lord loves everyone, even harlots like us. We had to give him thanks for watching over us while we were out there handling our business. We were making a thousand dollars or more each night, and we loved our new profession. There was never any feelings involved, just sex and money, and that's the way we liked it—no strings attached. Sometimes all we had to do was give a hand job, or listen while the johns talked our heads off. But whatever we had to do, the money was well worth it.

When Nina and I split up, our cell phones were always on. God forbid something happened while we were out there; we always had a secret code. Three rings meant this motherfucker is crazy and I got to go. Two rings meant I'm done, and meet me at the house. And one ring meant I'm going to be a little longer, and I'll meet you later on tonight. We only dealt with hustlers, and a lot of customers were friends of those hustlers from out of town. Our clientele was huge, and money was never a problem. I know you are saying damn bitch, tell us what kind of shit you and Nina did, well here it is.

Fat Sid was from Maryland, and he always wanted Nina and me together. He felt that his dick was so big he could fuck the both of us at the same time. He was four hundred pounds or more, and every time we were with him we tried, but we couldn't even get his dick up. But boy oh boy did we try! Our first night with him we entered his apartment to total darkness. He yelled for us to follow the music straight to the back of the house, and when we entered the room we were in for a sight.

Fat Sid was butt-naked, rubbing oil all over his massive body, and he was singing Shalimar's classic, "Make This a Night to Remember." Once he noticed us at the door, he waved us into the room and demanded that we strip. Once we were undressed we each took opposite ends of the bed and got busy. Nina took over his balls, while I went to work on his scrawny childlike penis. We sucked, licked, rubbed, bit, and spit, but nothing could give his fat ass an erection. It was a real sad sight, but he didn't care. He said we were the best lesbians he ever had, and started laughing.

Lesbians, I thought, *who the fuck is gay?* Instead of correcting his fat ass, all we could do was crack a smile, and wait for him to say that we were done. Once we were finished, we thanked Fat Sid, each of us kissing one of his jolly fat cheeks. And we took our money, and went home to wash his scent from our bodies. We each took three-hour baths after a night out, but after being with these men we never really felt to clean. But the money was right, so we kept going back.

One night I got a call to go meet this guy named Bernie Mack. No, not the actor, they just had the same name. He was a great big spender, too, but Bernie was a homebound dwarf. He was three foot eleven inches tall, but his dick was ten inches long. No shit, ten inches on a dwarf. All I could say was, wow! That shit looked crazy but Bernie was a true freak at heart, and he wanted every hole plugged that he could get. Our first meeting was real crazy, and believe me he was down for everything. When I got to his place Bernie was naked on the kitchen table, jerking his dick off, and it looked like he had a good rhythm going, too.

He gave me my money up-front and told me to undress and to lie down on the floor. I did as I was told, and he hopped off the table and went to work. He put his penis in my nose, ear, mouth and pussy, but he would not touch my asshole. When he was totally satisfied, he gave me the strap-on, twelve inches of rubber cock oiled up. He bent over, grabbed his ankles, and screamed for dear life while I fucked his asshole raw. When I was finished, Bernie curled up on the table, put his thumb in his mouth, and took his little ass to sleep just like a newborn baby. That was my cue to leave, and each time I went back shit was freakier than the last time.

Now Bony T was six-foot-three inches tall, and one hundred and fifty pounds soaking wet. He was very thin and so was his dick, and he only had one small testicle. All Bony T wanted was for me to jerk his dick and suck that one tiny ball. But if I stopped before he came I had to lick his ass with peanut butter and jelly until he reached his climax. Go figure, right, so it would be in my best interest not to stop until he reached his goal, and sometimes it could take awhile.

With all those nasty motherfuckers we were dealing with, you know we had to stay in the free clinic on 137th Street and Fifth Avenue. Doctor O'Connor kept a close watch over us. She knew what we were out there doing, and she said if we were not going to stop at least she could keep us safe. She made sure Nina and I had condoms, both male and females. We were on birth control pills, because there would be no children for us until we were married, and who knows when that would be.

We had just pulled an all-nighter and I was very tired, so when someone started banging on my apartment door it scared the shit out of me. I jumped out of bed and wondered who the hell would be ringing my bell at 7:00 AM. It took me awhile to get to the door, and by now whoever was out there was not only banging, they were also kicking on my motherfucking door, too. I yelled, "Who the fuck is it?"

The person responded, "It's me."

I yelled back, "Who the fuck is me?"

"It's me, Ty."

"Ty who?"

"It's Ty, your sister's man! Now, Jazz, open up the fucking door."

I opened the door and before I could say another word Ty pushed his way inside. I was standing there in total shock with my mouth hanging open, wondering what drug this nigga was on. When I got my bearings together I started saying, "Shonda's not here, I think she went to work already."

And that bastard looked me straight in my eyes, and said, "Yeah, I know. I already dropped little Ty off at the babysitter, and Shonda's off at work, but that's not why I'm here. I'm here to see what's up with you, Jazzy Jazz." He had an evil smirk on his face.

"What's up with me, motherfucker? I was sleeping, that's what's up, and I don't even rock with your ass like that so what the fuck do you want?"

Ty started screaming, "You fucking slut, you bitch," then he punched me in my mouth, grabbed me by my hair and dragged me into my bedroom.

At this point I was scared as shit. What the fuck was wrong with this nigga? Ty had done some sick shit like grabbing my ass and pinching my breasts when Shonda wasn't looking, but he had never done anything like this before. All I thought was this motherfucker had lost his damn mind, and one of us was going to die today. Then he stood over me rubbing himself, saying, "You fucking slut, you're already fucking everybody else and now I am here for my turn! You know you always wanted me, so don't fight it and stop all that damn crying!" I don't know why I didn't scream, I know I should have but I just didn't.

I'm not going to lie I was scared to death, and when he penetrated me with so much force I thought I would die from the pain alone. I don't know where the voice came from, but I heard it clear as day. It said, "Look under your pillow," and then I knew what I had to do, and at that point Ty should have been scared, too! Because I never go to sleep without my scalpel under my pillow and everyone who knows me knows that. When Ty jumped on me one of his hands was holding my hands up, and the other one was around my throat. After he raped me for twenty minutes nonstop my chance finally came. Ty screamed out that he was coming, and he loosened his grip on me.

I took my chance and out came Mary—my scalpel—and before I realized what had happened, Ty's neck was cut wide the fuck open and there was blood squirting everywhere. All I remember was screaming bloody murder and seeing the color red. Somehow I must have blacked out. When I came to Wella and Nina were standing over me yelling my name. I looked to the side, hoping that it was all a bad dream, but my worst fears were confirmed. Ty was lying very still, and there was so much blood, and Wella kept asking me over and over again what happened. I tried to open my mouth but I couldn't talk. All I could do was cry. Wella and Nina stayed with me until Shonda came home from work, and as the police, ambulance, and coroner came all I could do was cry. The police took my statement, and then I was taken to Harlem Hospital so they could do a rape kit and collect their evidence for their case.

The only reason I wasn't being charged with murder was because Ty had also raped a neighbor in his building over the weekend. Her name was Jackie and she was fifteen years old, and Ty was being sought for questioning ever since Friday night. The police were calling my case self-defense, but said I may be needed later for further questioning at the precinct. The rape kit was finally finished, and then the doctor told me that I was done, I could go home. The home where I was brutally destroyed, violated like a whore in the fucking street. And then it hit me like a ton of bricks. My chest got real tight, and I could not breathe. I realized that I was a whore, and that was the first time that I had acknowledged it. I felt like shit on a stick, and I still had to deal with Shonda when she got in.

When we got back to Wella's house she washed me up and made me a sandwich. I wasn't hungry, so we went back to my house to wait for Shonda. By then the coroners had already taken Ty's body away, so all we could do was sit and wait. All I kept asking myself was, what was Shonda going to say when she finally got home, and what was taking her so long? Wella had called her hours ago.

When Shonda and little Ty came in, Wella told Nina to take little Ty next door so we could talk in private. Shonda looked around and asked us what was going on. We said nothing. All I could do was cry, and say I'm sorry over and over again. At this point Shonda was scared. Wella had only told her it was an emergency, and that she had to come home. Not knowing what was going on, Shonda had a nervous look on her face, and her face was getting real pale.

Wella said, "Shonda, sit down, we have something very important to tell you."

"Wella, I don't want to sit down, please just tell me what the hell happened here."

"Okay, Mommy, I will tell you, but you may need to sit down first."

Shonda started screaming, "Will somebody just fucking tell me what the hell is going on?"

"Shonda, Tyrone is dead, I'm sorry."

"What did you just say? Ty ain't dead. You're wrong, Wella, who told you that bullshit? He dropped me off at work this morning, so he can't be dead."

"Shonda, Ty raped Jazmine this morning, and she cut his throat defending herself."

All I remember is Shonda screaming no, and me hitting the floor. Shonda attacked me immediately. She was punching and kicking me, calling me a fucking slut and every other name in the book. She was saying she always knew I wanted Ty, then she screamed, "Jazmine, you are finished here!" All I could do was cover my face. I just curled up in a tight ball and prayed that this assault would stop soon. I took all the hits that she gave me, and I just cried. I was to weak to do anything else. When she was finished, Shonda told me to pack up all my clothes and get my whoring ass out of her house. I was motherless and homeless, and getting paid for sex did not look so appealing to me after I was violated and raped.

Chapter Three

On My Own

I was listening to Patti Labelle's greatest hits, and her lyrics were filling me up all the way to my soul. I still couldn't believe I was really on my own, that things had ended up this way. I knew this wasn't how it was supposed to be. Patti had a different meaning when she sang her song, but it's all the same concept, everything that's happened in my life has a meaning. Take my mother's boyfriend Sammy raping me—when I told my mom about it she laughed right in my face.

She said, "If your fast ass weren't always walking around here half-naked all the damn time, Sammy would not have wanted your grown ass! Now you saying he raped you, you stupid white bitch. You wanted it, I can see it all over your fucking face." Then she slapped the shit out of me. When the first tears formed in my eyes she slapped me again and again. Then she started beating me, like I was a stranger in the street. That's the only other time I blacked out, and when I came to once again, Nina and Wella were standing over me calling my name.

My mother was screaming, and yelling, "she told Wella get this slut bag whore out of my house now." But all I could hear was, "I hate you, Jazmine, you were my worst mistake. I should have gotten rid of you seventeen years ago, when your bastard of a father raped me. Shit, I always knew you would be trouble, and now my worst fear has come true! Now you can get the fuck out, and don't you bring your white ass back here for as long as I'm alive and breathing." As I tried to pick myself up to go and pack my stuff, she yelled out, "And don't you take a motherfucking thing I brought your white trifling ass either. Don't take anything I brought you, I mean it, and you know I'm watching your ass."

Wella just looked at me on the cold tile floor. I was bloody, broken, abused, and ashamed. And all she could do was shake her head as a tear fell from her eye. Nina came over to me, picked me up, and led me out the door. The last words I ever heard my mother say to me or anyone else was, "I hope you drop dead, you white bitch, and good riddance." as I walked away hurt, all I wondered was how could I ever expect my mother to love me when I didn't think she ever really loved herself?

My mother, Tracey Roberts, was born to Janice and Vernon Roberts in Charlotte North Carolina on May 1, 1948. She was an only child, and her family didn't have much money, so they were very poor. Her father could not handle the pressure of providing for his family, so he took my grandmother's life on one cold and lonely day. Then he ended his own life with a fatal gunshot wound to the head. When my mother returned home from school that day, she found her mother and father lying side-by-side on the floor in their bedroom.

Next to their dead bodies was the note her father had written and left for her. In the letter her father apologized for all the sorrow she had to endure in her short life on this earth. He wrote that there was five hundred dollars hidden in the kitchen cabinet. And there was also a bus ticket to New York City under their bedroom mattress. He wished her well in her new life, and then he ended the letter by saying that he and her mother loved her dearly.

My mother finally pulled herself together and realized that she had no family left in her hometown. She wasted no time, leaving the only home that she ever knew with her meager belongings. When she reached the big city of New York she knew not a soul and fell into a very bad crowd in Harlem. Not long after that she fell in love with a very bad man named Danny who would later turn out to be Shonda's father. Danny was into a little bit of everything, and he was killed in a robbery gone bad two years after my sister was born. My mother tried to raise my sister up right, but with so many obstacles in her way it seemed like she was destined to fail.

By now she was hooked on heroin, and she became known for selling her body for her next fix. She did try to keep my sister clothed and fed, but at times it did get very hard for them to stay afloat. So for the next four years my mother was out in the streets, doing anything and everything to stay high. On one of her many missions she ran into the man who would later become my father. His name was Bernard, and she knew him from 138th Street and Eighth Avenue. He was living here and there with many different women, and had children spread throughout the five boroughs. Just like the Temptations sang, Bernard was a rolling stone. He never claimed any of the children he helped produce over the years. He was just like any other man out there in the street. Lying, cheating, and telling the women that he came across all the shit he felt they wanted to hear. It was all lies. A month after they met, he raped my mother because she was disrespectful to him in front of his so-called friends. She wouldn't have sex with him the way he wanted her to. Bernard wanted to fuck her in her ass and she was not having it. He felt disrespected by her telling him no, so he violated her in every hole she had, and nine months later that rape produced me. When Wella called Shonda to come and get me after my mother put me out, I felt so alone. I felt that the direction my life was taking would kill me in the end.

God when would this end? I was fifteen and my life wasn't worth a pile of shit! Shonda had moved out five years ago, because she and my mother could not get along. She moved in with Ty, so she was not around to see all things that Sammy was doing to me. Maybe if she lived at home things would have turned out differently for me. But she didn't live at home, and that shit worked out the only way it could—for the worst. Now once again, I'm back at Wella's house, only this time I have no one to call to come and pick me up.

I never knew my father, but the story my sister told me was sick, twisted, and tragic. She told me my father was just another disgusting, perverted bastard who liked molesting and sodomizing little girls. He was murdered when my mother was five months pregnant with me for raping and killing his girlfriend's seven-year-old daughter, Ebony. Before the police could catch him, the girlfriend's brother caught him first.

Pow Wow was her brother's name, and when he tracked that bastard down he tortured him for a full week in his house. Then he gutted him like a fucking fish, and left him on his mother's stoop wrapped as a gift. When his mother saw his dead, battered corpse, she collapsed and died from a heart attack that very same day. Years later when I heard the story on the street, I wasn't really shocked because Shonda had already told me. You know how the streets love to talk, but some of the stories you hear out here are actually true. All I could say was farewell to Bernard Julies Perkins, my father who I never knew. Farewell to a grandmother I will never have. And like my mother said to me on that sad day when she took her man's side over mine, "Good riddance."

I had been living with Nina and Wella for two weeks, and after going to the police prescient several times, my rape case was finally closed. Thank God that I was still a juvenile, because now my case file would be sealed just in case I ever got into any more trouble in the future. I had not seen Shonda and little Ty since the day that I was raped, but I knew that bastard Ty's funeral was the day before. Of course I didn't go, I did not think I could handle it. I really missed my nephew but when I called the house to talk to him and Shonda heard my voice, she hung up on me. I couldn't eat since that day. Wella and Nina kept telling me that I had to pull myself together, but how could I?

Wella said, "Mommy, I know it's hard, but it's been two weeks and you have to shake it off."

Nina kept saying, "Jazz, everyone's asking about you, and you know you need this money now more then ever. Come on, let me set up some dates for us, come on, Jazz, what do you say?"

I looked over at Wella, and then I looked at Nina and said, "Whatever. If it doesn't kill me, it would only make me stronger, right?" And then I thought, one could only hope for the best in this world. I had no family besides Nina and Wella, and I was really on my own, so I had to take my life back. That night Nina and I met up with Tyrell and Mink, and that night changed my life forever. They were two cats from Queens who we met through some dudes from Brooklyn. Tyrell and Mink had money coming out their ass. They had Queens on lock, and any money that came through their borough they had their hands in that shit!

That night we went to Carmine's, an Italian restaurant in lower Manhattan. Then we went to a hotel in New Jersey called The Globe that we heard was very upscale. From our conversation at dinner, I knew that Mink had a good head on his shoulders, and he was not a lame-ass dude. We got a suite with two rooms, and from the time our door closed I felt a connection with him that I could not explain. Mink was sitting on the bed looking at me, and then he patted the spot beside him, and asked me to come sit next to him. I don't know why I was afraid, but I felt something that I could not explain, and I did not like the feeling at all.

Mink kissed me very gently, and I swear I saw stars all around. In my profession kissing was a no can do, so I don't know why I did not stop him. I can't explain what came over me, but I was not going to fight it. After that kiss Mink undressed me, and laid me down gently on the red satin sheets. Then he took off his clothing, and he kissed every surface of my body with soft gentle pecks. When he got to my love box, I lost all control. Never in my life had I felt stimulating sensations like I did that night. Mink was my savior, and he ate me like it was his last meal on earth. I counted seven orgasms before everything became a blur. When Mink entered my nest, I screamed in pain and delight. He had to be twelve inches or more, and I took every last inch like my life depended on it.

There are 101 or more sex positions in the world, and I swear we tried them all that night. Mink had me in missionary, doggie style, Indian style, standing up, anal, upside down, and on a chair. I rode Mink front and back cowgirl style, we fucked like there would be no tomorrow. We made so much noise my voice was hoarse, but I could not get enough of that dick. After we bonded for five mind-blowing hours, Mink was out cold, but I could not sleep. I just stayed up for awhile longer thinking, asking God about my life and what was in store for me.

After that magical night, Mink started calling me on a regular basis. We talked about anything and everything under the sun, and I was honest with him and upfront about what I did for a living. Which was selling my body to any man who was offering the right price. It was funny because nothing I did or said seemed to bother him. He just did not seem to care about any thing in my past, and I was alright with that.

One day he told me that he saw something special in me. He said he was going to make an honest women out of me if he had to die trying. He was always asking questions about my goals, and what I wanted to do with my future.

He said, "I want to know the real Jazmine."

I told him, "When you find her, please give me a call and let me know."

He laughed, and said, "Girl, you got jokes."

"Only when the situation calls for it," I replied.

As the weeks wore on we were still talking every night, and we were getting pretty serious real fast. My better judgment told me to stay away from him—you know that inner voice that we all have. Don't get me wrong, Mink was everything any women would want. He had a dark chocolate complexion, and he kept his hair in a low cut for his waves that were spinning out of control. He was five-foot-ten inches tall and he weighed 215 pounds He had sexy bedroom eyes that were dark brown, and the biggest dick known to mankind. He was thirteen inches long, and he knew what to do with what God gave him.

Mink had money galore, and he was very generous with it but something just wasn't right about him. He had real feminine ways, and at times, he would get real quiet on me. But my heart and soul said go for it, so I went for it. So even with my head screaming no, I put all my concerns to the side and started dealing with Mink exclusively. Mink and I were inseparable from the start, so that didn't leave much time for Nina and me to chill. Of course Nina was still out there doing her thing, and getting that paper. But that was my old life, and I was ready for a change.

When I told Nina I was giving up our lifestyle and going straight, she said fuck it. "If Mink does it for you and that's what you really want then go ahead, Mommy. Shit, he must be a warrior to keep that wet pussy of yours happy." I just shook my head and I bust out laughing, Nina was always saying some dumb shit. Honey was a clown, and she cracked jokes all day long. Then she said, "Fuck love and romance, give me a big dick and lots of money."

I looked at her and said, "Only big dicks."

She looked back and said, "Shit, if the nigger's money is longer then his dick, of course I will fuck him and make an exception. But he will have to pay triple." We laughed and laughed until tears came to our eyes, all in all it was a good night and I felt like my life was finally changing for the good. Six months into our relationship, Mink took me to meet his family and surprisingly everyone was cool. He had two brothers named Reggie and Man Man and a little sister named Miracle.

Man Man was three years older then Mink, and he was a bachelor who lived in Brooklyn. Reggie was two years younger, and he lived with his baby's mother Trina and their two kids in Queens, not too far from their parent's house. It was only boys until Miracle finally came along. Miracle was really a blessing for Mom and Pop Green. They were both in their late sixties, and Miracle was only eleven. They had wanted a little girl for years, but after having Reggie nothing happened, and just when they gave up hope here comes their tiny Miracle. They were the happiest family I had every seen in my life, and they made me feel right at home.

It was hard to believe that after all the gifts and trips that Mink had sprung upon me in our whirlwind romance, that a year had passed us by. We had traveled around the world and back, and it felt good to be treated like a real women instead of a whore. We went to Jamaica, and all the Virgin Islands that you can name. We went to Puerto Rico, Paris, London, France, Brazil, and Korea. I never thought my life would turn out like this, or that someone would love me this much except Wella and Nina. But I guess I was wrong, because I had finally found true love from a real man. I was always at Mink's house anyway so on our first anniversary when he asked me to move in with him, I wasn't shocked but I looked surprised anyway.

When he saw the expression on my face, he said, "Come on, ma, what's up? Make me a happy man, and say yes." In my heart I knew that I already loved him, so my mind was already made up.

So once again I took another big step, and whispered, "What the hell." I looked up at him with my answer, and with tears in my eyes I said, "Yes baby, I will move in with you."

Mink looked over at me with so much love in his eyes, pulled me to him, and said, "I love you, Jazmine."

With tears in my eyes I told him that I loved him too. That night we celebrated our new life together with a bottle of Cristal. We made love until the sun came up, and I knew that it could only get better from here.

Chapter Four

Changes

When I told Wella and Nina that I was moving out they were very happy for me, and they helped me pack up my things that same night. Wella said that it was time for a change in our lives, and she was happy that I got a second chance at a decent life. I felt like I was leaving the damn country, and I would never see them again. Even though I knew that wasn't the case, it still hurt to leave the only family that ever really loved me. Mink lived on Jamaica Avenue and 241st Street. It was a two-bedroom duplex condominium with one and a half bathrooms, and a nice view of the city.

Mink and I had been living together for two weeks when Tyrell came over for a visit. I know Tyrell was very upset about me moving in with Mink, but for the life of me I could not understand why. I didn't really know him, and we never said any unpleasant words to each other. I thought, "Who was he anyway? A nobody. So I told myself I would just keep my eye on him, and never get caught alone with that nut because who knows what would happen."

Tyrell was not as fine as Mink, but Nina told me the sex was off the charts. He was a big spender and he dressed nice, so I guess it was all good. But I still watched him like a hawk.

Mink and Tyrell were in the living room talking quietly, and when I was almost upon them I heard Mink say, "Tyrell, that's none of your fucking business, and now is not the time to talk about that shit anyway so don't bring it up again."

When I walked in the room Tyrell changed the subject, and he started telling Mink about all the money he was getting down in Virginia. Mink, being the money-hungry nigger that he was, had to jump head first back into the game. He had been chilling for a minute now, not selling drugs, but I knew from the look in his eyes that he was about to head out of town chasing that money.

They left to go out of town that same night. Before he left I told Mink that I didn't want him to go. But he's a man, and even though he loved me with all his heart, we needed money to survive.

In no time Mink had been gone for five weeks. I spoke to him every single day, sometimes more than once, and he was happy with the way the money was flowing. Mink and Tyrell were getting so much money it was crazy, but I wasn't anybody's fool.

If he sent home five thousand dollars, I only kept fifteen hundred and put the rest in the bank for a rainy day. Because you never know what might happen, shit it could rain tomorrow. Money was flowing, and for once in my life I felt like everything would be all right. Now eight weeks had passed and with Mink being gone, I was very lonely and in need of some companionship. I guess God must have heard my prayers, because he sent my homegirl to pop up for a long overdue visit.

Nina came to spend a few days with me at the right time. She tried to stay around since Mink was gone, but with her occupation sometimes it was hard. She knew Mink was out of town handling his business, and my best friend knew how lonely I could get. I was so happy to see her I could not contain myself, I hugged her for about ten minutes nonstop. Then we ate some Chinese food she had brought with her and we had a few drinks from my bar. After eating and having two drinks, we just sat back and talked about life.

All of a sudden Nina looked real sad and whispered, "Jazz, she's dying."

I was lost, so I asked her, "Nina, who the fuck are you talking about?"

She looks down and whispered real low, "Wella."

She was talking so low I had to ask her again, "Who?"

Nina looked me in my eyes, and with tears rolling down her cheeks she shouted, "Wella is dying, she has full-blown AIDS." She cried for a while, and then she said, "Jazmine, she's leaving me." Then she asked me what was she supposed to do?

That shit hit me hard, like a ton of bricks, and all I could do was put my head down and whisper a pray for Wella. Shit, after hearing that news there was nothing else for me to do, there was nothing left for me to say. I didn't realize tears were coming out of my eyes until I saw that my shirt was wet. This shit was real bad and all we could do was cry. When we got ourselves together long enough to talk, Nina told me Wella's sad story. This story I had never heard before, and I was in for a shock.

Wella Maria Gonzalez was born in San Juan Puerto Rico to Pedro and Mary Gonzalez. She was born on January 3, 1965, and she came into this world to poor living conditions. When Wella turned thirteen, her father decided that going to America would be a good move for his family, so they packed up their meager belongings to start a better life. Pedro had family that lived in Spanish Harlem on 110th Street between Madison and Park Avenue, and they were welcome to stay there as long as needed. Pedro's brother Ramon had left Puerto Rico ten years before, and he had established a good life for himself in the States. He was the superintendent of the building where he lived and he had a basement apartment, so his home was going to be their new home.

The one-bedroom apartment wasn't big enough for all of them, but living in San Juan was no better. The Gonzalez family finally made the move. They had been living with Ramon for six months when Wella's father found a job as a plumber. Wella thought things would get better. Soon she would find out how wrong she was.

Wella was fourteen years old, and she had made a lot of friends since moving to America. But out of all her friends, she was the closet to Carmen. Her crew consisted of three ride or die females who called themselves The Chica's. Carmen lived above Wella in the same building with her mother Diana. Carmen's mother's boyfriend Hector also lived in that apartment, along with her younger brother Carlos and her baby sister, Maria. Carmen was a good friend to have, and Wella and Carmen became close very quickly.

Wella's other friend's were Ada, Cynthia, and Rose. They all went to the same junior high school, P.S 108, between 107th and 108th Street and Madison Avenue. That was the place to be for the four little *bambinas*. They were all fully developed and looked older then their fourteen years, which got them into a lot of trouble all the time. Well into the school year Wella started dating a boy named Carlos, who lived around her way. Carlos was sixteen years old and very advanced for his age.

So of course their relationship got hot and heavy real quick, but Wella wanted to wait before she lost her virginity, and surprisingly Carlos was okay with her decision. All they did was kiss and hump, exploring each other's growing bodies. One day, Wella and Carmen were sitting on their stoop chilling, just shooting the breeze. After an hour Wella turned to Carmen and said, "Ce Ce, Uncle Ramon keeps looking at me with a strange look in his eyes. And it makes me feel very uncomfortable."

Carmen looked to be deep in thought. Then she said, "Mommy, if he comes at you, kick him in his balls real hard. Then hit him over the head with something, anything you can get your hands on. Wella, you have to fight back, never let anyone take advantage of you." Carmen looked away, and when she looked back into Wella's face she was crying. Carmen said, "I can give you this advice because I had to learn this same lesson the hard way."

Carmen told Wella that the year before she moved into the building she was grabbed off the street in broad daylight. She was coming home from school when she was abducted, and she was held captive for a little over a week. In that week Carmen was drugged, raped, sodomized, and left for dead by several different men. She didn't know who snatched her or why, but she was still going to counseling to get help with her issues. Carmen still had nightmares about what happened to her, and her shrink said she could have these dreams for years. All she could do was learn to cope with what happened and try to move on.

When she was done with her story they were both in tears. Wella asked Carmen why she had never told her about what happened before.

Carmen said, "We had just met, what was I supposed to say? Hi, my name is Carmen, and last year I was kidnapped and raped by several different men?" Then she looked at Wella and said, "What if I had told you, what would you have said?"

That was a hard question to answer, so Wella just sat there and said nothing at all. After a moment of silence, Carmen started making jokes about people who walked past their stoop. She was trying to break the tension that was so thick in the air, and her jokes worked. Wella and Carmen talked for a little while longer, then they laughed for the rest of the night. But the next day things were anything but a laughing matter, and nothing would be funny for Wella for a very long time.

Carlos walked Wella home from school that day, and her Uncle Ramon was on their stoop just like usual. When he saw them walking up, he said, "Wella, you're looking real pretty today in that dress!"

Wella stopped and said, "Hello, Uncle Ramon." Then she told Carlos that she would see him at school tomorrow, and she went into the building. Once inside her house, Wella put her coat and books away, and then she headed to the bathroom. As soon as she sat down on the toilet, Ramon barged into the bathroom. He snatched her up off the toilet by her hair, and started kissing her roughly. Wella was struggling to get as far away from him as possible, but in the small bathroom where could she go?

She was already pressed up tight on the wall by the doorway, and Ramon was very strong. Ramon was holding her so tight that there was nothing she could do to stop the assault that was happening to her. He must have weighed close to three hundred pounds, and he was breathing real heavy like a wild animal, and his breath stunk. Foam was coming out of his month, and he was rubbing all over Wella's young body. He was saying that he had waited for this day for a long time, and he could not wait to be inside of her.

Wella was very short, but she was developed beyond her age. She had a tiny waist, and her perky 34C breasts were irresistible. Her ass was unreal, and Ramon said that it was soft like a feather. Ramon was drunk and could not control himself, and all of that played a part in clouding Ramon's judgment that tragic day. Ramon would take his demons to the grave with him, and what he was thinking that day would remain a mystery to everyone involved.

He was still holding her very tight, and then he whispered in her ear, "I've been watching you for a long time, Mommy, and now the time has come. I want you to give me what you give that little bastard, Carlos."

Wella screamed and cried, "No, please, Uncle Ramon, don't do this! Please Uncle Ramon, you're hurting me."

Then he punched her with a closed fist in her face. With blood pouring out of her mouth she yelled out again, "Somebody please help me," but no one answered.

Ramon was very angry and agitated by now. He screamed, "I'm going to have this pussy, Wella, so stop fighting me." With a crazed look in his eyes, he told her to be a good girl or else he would kill her. He dragged her from the doorway with Wella kicking and screaming. He bent her small frame over the white porcelain sink, and laughed out loud. He was already hard with an erection, and he was jamming his fingers in her tight forbidden fruit. It was funny to Wella at that same moment, because she didn't notice until then that he was naked from the waist down.

All the noise she made went unheard. There was not a soul around to hear her cries. Ramon raped and sodomized Wella over and over again until she was left unconscious and bloody on the white bathroom floor. When he had finally satisfied his desire, Ramon left the apartment in a panic. He was nervous and jittery, looking for a place to hide out from the hideous crime he had just committed.

When Wella's father came home a few hours later he found his beautiful baby girl beaten and abused. She had been left for dead in a pool of blood on the cold linoleum floor. The police and ambulance arrived at the same time that her mother was coming home from work. When the paramedics brought Wella out of the building, her mother wondered what had happened. She knew it was something bad, because she had never seen her husband of sixteen years cry before.

Wella's parents rode with her in the ambulance to the hospital. They were with her for two days, and Wella had never regained consciousness.

There were many questions to be answered, and only she held the answers. The doctor said there was nothing else that they could do for her. All her parents could do was pray and hope for a miracle. On their third day at her bedside, their prayers were finally answered.

Wella awoke screaming, "No, Uncle Ramon, please, you're hurting me, somebody help me!" When the doctors rushed into her room and gave her a sedative, Wella calmed down enough to talk, and she told them her horrifying story. She told them every sick detail of her rape that she remembered, and as she told her story she relived every moment. She cried, begging her parents not to be mad at her. For some reason Wella felt that what happened was her fault, maybe she had asked for this to happen to her.

Her mother just cried, but Pedro was so upset that his blood was boiling—he started to lose control right then and there. Shortly after that, he left the hospital and brought a gun from a guy who he met through his job. Then he hopped on the number 2 train, and he went straight to the Bronx. He found Ramon at his girlfriend Jennifer's house, and shot him dead. Two shots to the head, he killed Ramon in cold blood, but he called it justice. Pedro was arrested that afternoon when he walked into the police precinct and confessed to his brother's murder.

He was charged with premeditated murder and possession of an illegal firearm. He felt that he did the only thing that he could do, an eye for an eye. His brother had raped his daughter, and he had to die. For the violation of his baby girl, Pedro did what he felt was right. He had a bail, but he told his wife not to worry about paying it. He said that he would just sit in jail awaiting his fate, and for her not to worry about him. All Pedro asked of his wife Mary is that she take care of Wella.

As the months wore on Wella's body recovered, but her sanity did not. It was a very slow and painful process for her, and until the day that Wella died she had nightmares about what her perverted uncle did to her. Pedro had been in jail for seven months awaiting trial, but he had a good and caring public defender named Mr. Diaz. A man from their native country of San Juan, he told the Gonzalez family that he would get Pedro the best deal possible. Maybe no jail time at all because of his frame of mind at the time of the shooting.

Since the Gonzalez family had been in the country they had done nothing but work and save their money. Which was good for them, because now they would need that money to survive. Wella's mother was now the sole provider for her family. With the money they had saved, Wella and her mother were able to move into another apartment in the same building. The owner of the building felt bad about the tragedy that took place on his property, so he did a good deed and let them move upstairs into a vacant one bedroom.

Wella was home a lot by herself. Her mother had to work a lot of overtime to take care of her family. But no matter how tired she was, she tried to raise Wella up right. But Wella just felt empty inside. She didn't hang with her friends anymore, and she felt like there was nothing left to live for. She started sleeping with anyone and everyone; if you looked at her twice you were going to get some free pussy. As the months wore on, Wella started getting sick every morning. She was throwing up and she was always nauseous. Her mother didn't seem to notice because she was always at work, but changes had also started occurring in Wella's body. And before anyone realized it Wella was nine months pregnant, and there was nothing anyone could do about it.

On June 1, 1980, she gave birth to a beautiful, seven pound nine ounce baby girl she named Nina Simone Gonzalez. She named her Nina Simone after the famous singer, who was Wella's favorite. Three months after she gave birth to her darling daughter her father was found not guilty on all charges. The prosecution presented a strong case on behalf of the state, but after the closing argument of the defense, who could convict a father for trying to avenge his only child's rape?

I guess the jury knew when a man was hurting and just lost total control of a situation. Shit, that was his baby girl, and the defense asked the jury in his closing statement, "If she were your child, what would you have done?" They did the right thing, and released a good man who did an unfortunate thing. With Pedro coming home life could go on, which was a good thing, but it was too late for Wella. The streets had already sucked her in. She was using all kinds of drugs, and now she was selling her body for a no-good pimp named Flash Gordon. Wella met her new pimp not far from where she lived, and it was love at first sight. Flash Gordon, whose birth name was Jonathon Gordon, was an evil and conniving black son of a bitch. He only cared about himself, and how much money his hoes were bringing him.

When Wella first met Flash he told her that he would take care of her and make all of her pain go away. Little did she know that he would introduce her to dope, and once she was hooked on it she would do anything for her next fix. Shit, rumor had it that Flash Gordon's mother was a prostitute, and he was a trick's baby. I guess there are some things that we will never know, maybe that's why he was a pimp. As time went on, Wella could not handle the pressure, or the day-to-day struggle with living. She did not have the strength to go on. After all that was done to her in her young life she felt that she could not make it any longer.

She had to leave Nina with her mother and father, she said it was just until she could get herself together. Nina grew up in a stable home, and her grandparents treated her real well and they showed her nothing but love. At the tender age of five Nina got her first dose of reality. She lost her grandfather to a massive stroke. I guess the pain was so unbearable for her grandmother that she died less than a year later.

Nina was placed into the foster care system immediately, because there was no one around to claim this lost child. Even with never knowing her biological parents, and then losing her grandparents at a young age, nothing prepared her for the pain and heartache that she would have to endure for the next several years. She was left in the care of strangers who were supposed to show her love and kindness. These people were supposed to look after her and keep her safe from harm. In the years that followed, Nina was beaten, malnourished, raped, and sodomized. She was just all around the board abused, by adults who were supposed to know right from wrong, adults who were supposed to protect her.

It seemed like every foster home that Nina was sent to there was a perverted man waiting behind every closed door. All they wanted, besides the money for letting her live there, was her sweet young tender pussy, and there was no one to stop them from taking what they wanted. Her grandparents tried to raise Nina right, but a cruel twist of fate stepped in their way and they were taken from this earth to soon. The love that they bestowed upon their only grandchild before their untimely deaths stayed tucked somewhere deep inside of her. That's the only reason that Nina survived all the torture that was done to her throughout everything she went through in the fucked-up system.

In the foster homes all Nina ever did was stare at her mother's picture. Before she just *wanted* her mother to come and save her—now she needed her to come. She wanted her mother to take her away from this pain that she felt daily, before it was too late. She felt like she was losing control fast, and suicide was looking better to her with each passing day. Unknown to Nina, her mother was coming for her, but before Wella could show up on her parent's doorstep clean and sober they were both dead. Wella was finally in her right state of mind, ready to come and take back her daughter, but it was too late.

When she found out her parents were dead she cried for three days straight, but on that third day she dried her eyes because she knew what she had to do. Wella and her caseworker Ms. Turner worked long and hard to rescue Nina. Wella went to all the parenting classes and she completed all the courses that were required of her. She had to save her one and only child from sure death. When the caseworkers from child services asked Wella to explain how she could care for her child, she had something positive to tell them.

She explained to them that she had been in a drug program for the last fourteen months. She had completed it and also received her high school equivalent diploma while she was in there. She had recently moved into a two-bedroom apartment at 230 West 131st Street, between Seventh and Eighth Avenue in Saint Nicholas projects. She had a job at the drug program that she had just completed, and she was ready to bring her daughter home

She was granted full custody that same day. Now Wella, my mother, my mentor, and my friend, found out she has full-blown AIDS. She was going to die very soon, and there was nothing we could do about it. It was a very sad day for us. She overcame all that heartache in her life, and now her life was over in the blink of an eye

Chapter Five

Heartache

When Nina finished her story about the only mother who ever really loved and took care of me I was numb all over. All I kept thinking was, not my Wella. That weekend I went back home to stay with Nina and Wella before she was taken away from us forever. Wella was her old self—singing and dancing, dressing real sexy, and wearing makeup. But you could see the toll that the disease was taking on her body, and I was sick to death of all this heartache in our lives.

I stayed longer then I had expected to, and as the days wore on Wella seemed to become weaker and weaker. Right before our eyes, she became a sunken shell of her former self. She went from a size eight to a size two in a matter of weeks, and her hair started falling out. She could not hold any food or liquids down, and her bodily organs were shutting down on her one by one. We all knew the end was near, and there was no way to prevent this death that would shatter us for life.

On her deathbed, Wella finally told Nina the answer to the mystery that was surrounding the identity of her father. Nina had been asking this question ever since Wella rescued her from her living hell.

Wella looked over and grabbed her daughter's face in between her hands and said, "Nina, I'm sorry baby, but all these years I just could not answer your question. I could not look you in your eyes and tell you what you have always wanted to know.

"Now I have to tell you, and then maybe you will understand why I made so many mistakes in my life. And hopefully you will not destroy the life that you have left. Nina, I'm dying and I didn't even reach forty yet." By now Wella was crying and coughing, and she could barely get her words out. After a few minutes she mustered up enough strength to say,

"Nina, please don't make the same mistakes that I did. Try to avoid all the heartache that comes from making bad decisions. Please listen to me, both of yous, live your life to the fullest, and never give up on your dreams.

"You have a choice, baby, you have the right to choose different, don't believe what I said before, I taught yous wrong. Cherish your body and love yourself you have the chance to fix what I helped break. I didn't feel that I had a choice, and that's why I'm here today dying from AIDS." She looked away for a moment, took a deep breath, and than looked back at Nina and said, "I'm sorry, baby, but your father was my Uncle Ramon." Nina and I were both shocked, because when Wella told Nina the story of her past she made it seem like after the rape she was just promiscuous. Wella said there had been many different men, and that Nina's father could have been any one of them, but definitely not Ramon.

Nina was crying hysterically at this point, and as we both looked on with tears falling from our eyes, Wella coughed, and took her last breath in this cold and mean world. Life for Wella was hard but death came to her easy. At last, Wella Maria Gonzalez was at peace, and she went to meet her maker with a peaceful expression on her face. I assumed that she was finally at peace because she had finally told Nina the truth. The old folks say that the truth shall set you free, and I guess they were right. While I was dealing with Wella's illness I had completely forgotten about being lonely. With Mink's ass still out of town chasing that damn money I was staying right where I was. If Mink came home right now, I could not leave if I wanted to. I could not leave Nina alone at a time like this, and I did not like the look that she had in her eyes. It was vacant, empty, and sad, but I talked and talked until I finally convinced Nina to take the high school equivalent test. If we were going to get our lives together we needed something to look forward to. At least that would mean something positive was coming our way. Shit, maybe we could even go to college.

I spoke to Mink every day, and he sent me the money to pay for the funeral. He told me that we had to stay strong, and to keep our heads up. Of course he was still out of town chasing the almighty dollar, so he would not be home for the funeral, but he sent his love. Mink was sending me so much money that I was caked up, I had more than I needed, but the money didn't ease my pain. The dreaded day had finally arrived on May 11, 1996, Nina and I laid our beautiful mother to rest. Wella had a very peaceful look her face, and the entire service was exceptionally beautiful.

The service was at Unity Funeral Home in Harlem. They did a wonderful job on Wella, and Nina and I were both pleased with the turnout. After the service, Wella was buried in Woodlawn Cemetery in New Jersey. Nina took the loss of her mother hard, and my friend was hurting. She had become very withdrawn and angry toward me. I suspected that she was using drugs, but I had no proof. I only had a hunch and a bag of dope I found inside the couch.

With out me knowing it Nina had started using very hard drugs. She was hooked on crack. In the past we had smoked marijuana, even sniffed a little bit of cocaine, but that was the extent of it, and it only happened on special occasions. But heroin, now that was something else entirely. I had to find out what the hell was going on with her. I noticed that Nina had started staying out for days at a time, and when she was home all she did was sleep. While I was trying to get Wella's house in order, Nina was out there running the damn streets.

A few days later I was in the grocery store when a little nosy bird named Gloria whispered a few things in my ear. She said word on the street was that Nina was out there turning tricks for drugs. I was in shock. When we sold our bodies in the past it was for survival, now Nina was doing it for drugs. Somehow I had to put a stop to all this madness. I needed my man, but Mink was still out of town with Tyrell, hustling. I received my money every week like clockwork, but I had not seen him in over five months and I was lonely all over again.

One late night I heard Nina come in the apartment, and then I heard a loud thump out in the hallway. I got up to see what had happened, and when I turned on the hallway light I saw my worst nightmare. Nina, the only person besides Mink who I had in my corner, was lying in a pool of her own blood. She was sliced up and down her entire body. Surprisingly, she had no cuts or bruises on her face. It was so much blood I didn't know what to do, so I did the only logical thing that I could do. I dialed 911, and just waited, holding my sister who was dying in my arms.

When the police arrived they took my statement, and than we rode in the ambulance to Harlem Hospital. The ride over was scary. I cried the whole time, and the paramedics did not know if Nina was going to make it. When we reached the hospital Nina was rushed straight into the operating room, and I was left all alone with my fears. I waited for four hours, and after the surgery Doctor Palmer came out to talk to me about her condition. He told me if I had waited any longer to get her to the hospital, Nina would have died.

Nina had cuts on over 80 percent of her body, and she was raped repeatedly. Nina would never hear out of her left ear again, and she would never be able to bear children. I felt like someone had knocked the air out of me. I was hyperventilating, and I felt like I had to vomit. Doctor Palmer led me to her room, and all I could do was hold my sister's hand and cry. He told me it would take Nina a few months to recover, and then she would be as good as new. Yes, my friend's scars would heal, but I knew her mind would never be the same.

Nina was released from the hospital three weeks later. Two weeks after she came home I asked her what happened on the night that almost took her young life. She told me that she was getting high at a fiend's apartment on the eastside with all the other addicts. She said the last thing she remembered was taking a hit of dope, and the next thing she knew she was opening her eyes and she was in the hospital.

When I told Nina she was raped and could never have children, she looked at me, put her head down and said, "Jazmine, I am no longer afraid of anything. This is my fate." Then she closed her eyes and went to sleep. It was a slow recovery for Nina but her wounds were healing well, and she was in good sprits. Then six months after she was home, she started getting real sick. Nothing we did seemed to help, so I made her a doctor's appointment for a complete physical. Two weeks after her visit she was called back for an abnormal pap smear.

Once we arrived at the clinic, the doctor stated that that Nina's white blood count was very low, so he requested an HIV test immediately. That night after the test Nina lay in my arms and said, "Sis, I'm going to die just like my mother. Jazmine, it's my destiny, but always remember, I will always love and be with you." Nina drifted off to sleep soon after our conversation, and I was so very sad. I just held my sister, my friend. and cried myself to sleep. One week later we found out why Nina was forever sick. Nina was infected with the virus, the virus that causes AIDS.

Nina took the news pretty well, considering she was going to die some time in the near future, but Nina knew the truth even before her results came back positive. I, on the other hand, was a nervous wreck. Between making sure that Nina took all her medication, taking care of Wella's apartment, and keeping up with Mink, I was losing it. Thank God that the management office already had Nina's name on the lease to Wella's apartment, so she could keep it without a problem. I paid the rent up for a year, so that was taken care of and all Nina had to do was live. But I felt like I was dying a slow death, and I thought that I was having a nervous breakdown. I was there for everybody, but who would be there for me?

A few days later I was walking from the corner store when I ran into Shonda and little Ty. I wasn't going to speak at first, because Shonda was still acting like a real stupid bitch. At Wella's funeral she didn't even say hello to me or give me a hug. She just passed me by and kissed Nina on her cheek, whispering some words of encouragement in her ear. I was still hurt and upset with her, but when my nephew ran toward me yelling my name, "Auntie Jazz, Auntie Jazz," all my anger flew up and out of me.

All I could do was open my arms real wide, and got ready for a great big hug. Shonda walked over to us with her hands on her hips and said, "Hello, Jazmine," and all I could do was stare at her. Shonda had the nerve to roll her eyes at me, as if I was the one that was in the wrong. I guess little man was trying to break the tension, because little Ty said, "Auntie Jazz, where have you been? I've missed you."

With tears rolling down my eyes I told him that I missed him too. I said, "Little man, Auntie has been very busy, but whenever you want to speak to me, just ask your mother to call me and I'll be right there."

I gave my nephew one more hug, told him that I had to go, but promised him that I would see him real soon. With tears in my eyes I turned away from them, but Shonda grabbed my arm and said, "I'm so sorry, Jazz, please don't leave. I was wrong for putting you out over Tyrone, will you please forgive me?" I was shocked, but before I could get my thoughts together, a car pulled up and out jumped four females. I wasn't worried about it, though, because I didn't know them, and just when I went to turn back around to talk to Shonda, I noticed that they were running right toward us. All I had time to do was push little Ty back on the gate around the building and start swinging. We fought for about twenty minutes, and all I heard was little Ty screaming. I wondered where all the nosy people were at who were always in the front of the building minding everyone's business.

Just when I thought things could not get any worse, I heard gun shots ring out. All I saw was gun smoke around me, and everything else was just a blur. When I looked up, Shonda was holding a chrome .380 handgun and tears were falling from her eyes. When I looked to my left, Shonda had shot two of the bitches that we were fighting, and the other two were dragging their friends to the car trying to hightail it out of there. They were trying to get the hell out of dodge. I was standing there in shock with my mouth hanging open, stunned into silence, when Shonda grabbed me by one arm and little Ty by the other and dragged us into the building.

Thank the Lord that the elevator was working, because I would not have been able to make it up the stairs. When we got in the house, little Ty was still crying, so Shonda took him to the back to settle him down, and I was left all alone to get my emotions in order. I slid down to the ground, laid my head back and just closed my eyes. Not knowing how long I sat there, my mind was going around in circles. One crazy thought after another kept running through my mind, and I was very confused.

When I finally looked up, Shonda was standing over me yelling out my name. She pulled me up and led me over to the couch to sit down.

Don't get me wrong, I am nobody's punk, and I have seen guns before. Shit, I have even seen people murdered. But never in a million years would

I have thought that stuck-up Shonda would have a gun and not be afraid to use it. Just when you think you know someone, you find out that you don't really know him or her at all. Not Shonda who would never even get loud with a nigger, not Shonda who when we were younger would not fight back even if her life depended on it.

I looked over at Shonda and asked, "What's the deal? Who were those bitches, and where did you get that gun?" She looked away from me, but before she turned her head I saw the tears falling from her swollen eyes. Shonda turned back to face me and for the first time, I saw the blood all over her brown shirt. I realized that she was hurt and one of those bitches had sliced her shoulder wide open. I was really pissed the fuck off, one of those bitches cut my sister.

I knew we had to go to the hospital to get Shonda examined, so I called Nina to come over. I told her what happened outside, and than I asked her to watch the little man. Nina said no problem, and she was there in a matter of seconds. She walked in and we walked out, and headed straight to the emergency room at Harlem hospital. It must have been God watching over her because the cut was not as deep as I first thought that it was, and she only needed ten stitches. They gave her some pain medication, and told her that her wound would heal in due time.

When we got back to the house Nina and little Ty were fast asleep in his bed, so we left them that way. Shonda and I were both tired, so we did not get a chance to talk about what went down earlier that day. We just laid down and went to sleep, but we would have this conversation sooner then later.

Chapter Six

Revelations

The next morning I dressed little Ty and took him to the babysitter up the block from our building. I also called Shonda's job and got her some time off from work. I told her boss that we had a family emergency and had to leave town immediately. Now it was time for me to find out what the hell was going on with those bitches from yesterday. I waited for a few hours, and then I went into Shonda's room. She was lying there just staring at the ceiling, so I called out to her.

I asked her, "Are you hungry?"

"No, Jazz, I'm okay."

"Are you sure? You know you have to eat something."

Shonda looked over at me with a sad look in her eyes and said, "Jazz, I'm not hungry, so please just stop asking me."

I said, "Okay, Sis," then I took a seat on the edge of her bed. We sat like that for a while in total silence, and then Shonda started talking out of nowhere. The revelations that spilled out of her mouth chilled me to the bone.

"Jazz, that was Tyrone's other baby mother and her sisters."

I was sitting there losing my mind, because to my knowledge Ty didn't have any more children. So I asked her, "What the fuck do you mean his other baby mother? Where did she come from?"

"They got together, and started fucking around over a year ago. It was around the same time we broke up. Do you remember the time when Ty busted my lip, and took my keys so I could not leave the house?" she asked.

"Yeah, I remember that bullshit."

"Well, anyway, we were only separated for about three months, but I guess that's all it takes for a man to find a replacement."

Now all I was thinking is that nosy bitch Gloria from down the street did tell me a while ago that she saw Ty with some girl from 135th Street and Lenox Avenue named Latrell. Shit, at that point in time Ty could do no wrong in Shonda's eyes. So I figured if she didn't care what her man was doing or who he was fucking, than neither did I. I brought up my conversation with Gloria and to my surprise Shonda said she already knew about it. I asked her how she found out.

She said that she saw them together on 125th Street one day, but at the time she was still angry and acted like she didn't even notice them. She said when they got back together she asked him about the girl, and just like a man he lied about Latrell.

"He lied right to my fucking face, Jazz, and just like a damn fool I fell for that bullshit, and all the other lies he filled my head with at the time."

That was the first part of Shonda's story, and the rest of it was just as bad.

Shonda said, "The day before Ty raped you, little Ty had a doctor's appointment at Mount Sinai Hospital on One Hundredth Street and Fifth Avenue. While we were sitting there waiting to be called, Latrell and some other chick walked in. She was carrying a little girl in her arms, no older then nine months, and they took a seat on the other side of the waiting room. We were all sitting there for a while when Latrell walked over, parked her stroller, dropped the baby in Ty's lap, and then walked away like everything was fucking normal. Now, Jazz, you know the expression that was on my face was one of shock, so I asked Ty what the fuck was going on? Who was that girl—is that your fucking baby?" Then Shonda looked at me and said, "That lying bastard had the nerve to say, 'Now baby girl, you know this is not my baby. That was just Latrell, a friend of mine from around the way.' Then he said, 'And once again, just for the record, no, this is not my baby.' You know I flipped the fuck out right?

"Jazz, I was really going crazy by then, because I felt like that motherfucker was trying to play me. I was a fool up until that very moment but no more, my fantasy world had just turned to reality. I was screaming and going crazy, and Ty was screaming too, trying to flip all this bullshit on me. Little Ty and the baby were crying, and the receptionist behind the desk said that she was calling security. When security finally arrived, they escorted us out of the building and told us that we could come back in after we both settled down.

"When I looked to my left, that slim bitch Latrell was standing there laughing her ass off. She and her friend, who had on the green short set yesterday, had followed us outside. They were laughing in my face. As soon as the toy cops went back inside, looking back like they were protecting somebody, I flipped out again. I punched Ty right in his lying face, and just kept on swinging. That punk bitch Latrell waited until Ty had me pinned on the ground, and then she ran over and kicked me in my head. Then that bitch grabbed her daughter, and they jumped in the same car that rolled up on us yesterday.

"Jazz, I was so fucking mad, I just grabbed Little Ty's stroller and started walking home." When I came in the house, Ty was already here sitting on the couch talking on the damn phone like everything was all right. When he realized I had walked in he hung up real fast, comes over, picks up little Ty and undresses him and acts like everything is okay. The nigger had the nerve to ask me what we were having for dinner. I just walked in my room and slammed the damn door. Two hours later I'm still sitting in my room trying to collect my thoughts, when I heard the first door slam shut.

"I went in the living room, and of course Ty was gone. I did not believe that he had the audacity to just up and leave with all this shit that was going on. I don't know what time I went to sleep that night, all I remember is sitting up and the next thing I know the alarm clock was going off at six. I dressed little Ty and myself, dropped him off at the sitter's and went to work. When I came home Ty had raped you, you sliced his throat, and he was dead.

"I'm sorry that I did not believe you, but my emotions were going every which way anyway and I just took it out on you." We were both crying at this point, and Shonda kept asking over and over again, "Little Sis, please forgive me, I'm so sorry, please forgive me?" After we got out all the tears and pulled ourselves together, I looked over and my cell phone was going off like crazy. It must have rung like thirty times or more, and I was sick of it going off. When I finally checked my voicemail, Mink had left me twenty messages from an out-of-town number one that I did not recognize.

When I called the number back, some dude answered the phone. I said, "Hello, can I please speak to Mink?"

He put me on hold and yelled out, "Mink, some chick is on the phone for you," and then he dropped the receiver with a loud bang.

When Mink finally came on the line he shouted, "Who is this?"

I said, "Baby it's me, what's up?"

"Oh hey, baby. I've been calling you all day. Is everything okay with you?"

I was very quiet for a few seconds, and when I opened my mouth everything that had happened over the last few days just came spilling out.

Mink listened quietly while I talked, and when I was done he just kept saying the same thing over and over again.

"Baby, calm down, everything is going to be okay. I promise everything will be just fine."

In the background I heard someone yelling, "Mink, get off the damn phone, you over there making love, nigga, we have things to do!"

Mink said, "Alright, son, hold your head, I'm talking to my wife, just give me another minute." Then he said, "Ma, I have to go and handle some business with my dudes but keep your head up, and I will call you later. Everything will be all right I'm sure of it, and I promise that daddy will be home soon."

I said, "Alright, boo, be safe and I love you." He said he loved me too, and then we hung up. I was on the telephone for a while, and when I went back in Shonda's room she was crying all over again. There was nothing I could do to ease her pain, so I just held her until she calmed down again. Nina called a little while later and asked what we were doing. I told her nothing, just relaxing. She said she was on her way to the building, and asked did we want her to go and get little Ty from up the block? I told her yes, that would be great, and I asked could she bring up something to eat. Nina said she was going to the supermarket first, and then she would be on her way. I thanked her and we hung up.

That night we had a quiet dinner, chilled, and got some much-needed rest. Even little man didn't fight his sleep; for once even he was tired. The next morning, Nina took little Ty to the sitter for us, she said she would see us later on this evening because she had something important to do. Nina had been doing okay mentally, and she was taking her medication on a regular basis. She was handling her disease like a trooper would; she was making all her doctor's appointments and she had even left the drugs alone. She was no longer selling her body for her next fix, and she was respecting herself. At least I did not have to worry about her for the moment, or so I thought.

Nina and I had taken our GED test a couple of months after Wella had passed away, and I was very nervous waiting for our test results. I knew we were both smart, so I knew we passed with flying colors, but I was still thinking negative. I actually thought when our test scores came back our life would finally be on the right track, at least I hoped for the best. Nina and little Ty left the house at eight thirty that morning, so all Shonda and I did was lounge around the house all day. We watched all the talk shows and the soap operas we loved.

All My Children and *One Life to Live* were the best soap operas ever invented. When I was caught up in their twisted lives I didn't have to think about the many problems I was having in my life. At four o'clock we finally got dressed and went to pick up little Ty from the babysitter. The ringer had been off on the telephone all day, so when we came back in Shonda went to turn it on while I went to the kitchen to fix us something for dinner. As soon as the telephone was turned back on the crank calls started.

The stalkers called nonstop, and they did not stop until we turned the ringer back off at midnight. Shonda said it was Latrell and her friends, she said they did that same dumb shit right after Ty first died. So we just tried to ignore it, but the shit they were saying was crazy. They said they were going to kill Shonda and her fucking bastard son. They said that threat went for anyone else who wanted to get involved with this shit, they could get it too.

I mean they did that shit all fucking night. Do you hear what I am saying—all fucking night! Damn they didn't have anything else to get into? Where the fuck was their dick or anyone else's dick for that matter? I guess there was nothing else to do, because they did not stop until we got fed up and cut the damn thing off again. The next morning, after we dropped little Ty off at the babysitter, Shonda and I walked to the corner store to get some breakfast. I was starving. I knew we ate dinner the night before, but my stomach was acting like it did not remember.

At the store we ran into David, aka Black. He was this dude we grew up with from our building. When Black noticed us, he said, "What's good, Jazz and Shonda, what's up?"

We both replied, "Nothing, Black, what's good with you?

He said, "Chilling, just sticking and moving, you ladies know how I do." Laughing we said, "Yeah, we know how you do." We clowned around for a little while longer with Black, and it felt good.

I was so happy to see Shonda laughing, and smiling, I was really worried about her for a minute, and I just wanted her to get her life back on track. At that moment I looked over my shoulder, and saw these two tack head broads named Stacey and Linda who lived up the street from us. Nina and I did not like them, and they did not like us either. Of course we fucked some dudes that they were dealing with, so there was no love lost between the four of us. It was nothing personal, just business.

As we got our food and started to leave the store, I heard Linda say, "Bitches are out here fucking anything and everything that moves. Shit, hoes better watch their back."

I looked over my shoulder and said, "My back is always being watched, bitch. Nina is never too far behind me."

Then that bitch Stacey said, "Shit, Nina is out here strung out on drugs, fucking little boys, dogs, and anything else just to get her next fix. So bitch, please."

When I say I was pissed the fuck off I am not lying. Words could not describe how I was feeling. I was just standing there in shock, and then those tricks bumped me hard and walked out of the store.

I was very angry at what I just heard, but I was more worried then anything else. Nina had stopped spending the night out weeks ago, but she did not come home the night before. All I was thinking was, *Where the hell is Nina, and what has she gotten herself into now?*

Chapter Seven

Confessions

Three weeks passed, and I was scared because I still had not seen or heard a word from Nina. No one on the block had heard from her either, and I knew what those bitches said was true. I filed a missing person's report at the police station after she had been gone for five days. All those bastards said to me was they would do their best. Who did they think they were talking to, boo boo the fool or somebody?

What the fuck was their best? They could not even find Bin Laden who terrorized our goddamn country for several years. I could not wait on their slow asses forever, so I took matters into my own hands and hit the streets. I went from uptown to downtown, across town and back around again. I went to all our old stomping grounds, and believe me we had a lot of them. I saw a lot of familiar faces, guys who hadn't seen me in over a year. Everybody I came across was asking the same question, and making the same comments

"Jazmine, where the hell have you been, girl?"

"Shit, but wherever you been, stay there, because girl its doing your body good." I would just laugh and say, "I've been around. You know just doing the things that I like to do." and everyone I came in contact with I asked him or her the same question.

"Hey, have you seen Nina around here?"

Everybody gave me the same exact answer, "No little Sis, I haven't seen her in weeks." I was starting to get very discouraged and depressed. It seemed like Nina had disappeared into thin air.

I went by Shonda's house, who by the way was doing wonderful. She had a new man in her life named Michael, and I must say he was a cutie.

He's very tall, with a buff build like a body builder. It seemed like all he did was work out at the gym, but I wasn't mad at him.

He had the most beautiful set of bluish-green eyes you have ever seen on a full-blooded black man, and all I could say was goddamn. Shonda and Michael had worked together for the past three years, but they had just started dating. He has been trying to get to know Shonda a little better for over a year now, but with all the drama that was going on in her life she was not ready for romance. Then out of nowhere she decided to cut him some slack, and give him a chance, and it was off to the races from there. Michael was also crazy about my nephew, little Ty, and I felt that in the long run they would be a very happy family, so it was all good with me.

It took a few months after we had the fight, but the crank calls finally stopped. That was only because Shonda finally changed the telephone number. Shonda did not want to change the number, because she has had the same number ever since she moved back into the apartment right after my mother's murder, but what else could she do? What finally convinced her, though, was her coworker Tanya. Tanya had been in a similar situation as Shonda.

She told Shonda in order for her to move on with her life she would have to do what she had to do to save her sanity. If those bitches calling her house were driving her that crazy, she had to change her number. The next thing I knew Shonda was giving me a new telephone number, and now everything was all good again.

I had just arrived at her place, and I sat down on the couch to relax my tired and aching bones. Damn I was tired. My body felt like I had been walking around for weeks, and then the light bulb in my head went off. Dummy, you have been walking around for weeks. Just as I had settled on the couch and closed my eyes to rest them, somebody knocked on the damn door.

I looked through the peephole and it was India, this chick who lived upstairs with her daughter, Asia, and her man, Benny. Nina and I were always cool with India, ever since we went to junior high school together. I also knew she kept some good weed at all times, so I was happy to see her. But when I opened the door and saw the expression on her face, I knew something was terribly wrong. Sister girl always had a smile on her face, and she was always a pleasant person to be around. As soon as she walked in she said, "Jazz, I need to talk to you about something important."

"Sure, friend, what's up?"

"Do you know who Gloria is?"

"Who, nosy Gloria from up the block? Yeah, I know her, why?"

"Well, she told me that she saw Nina sliding with Benny the other night."

"What Benny—your Benny?" She nodded her head yes.

Then I said, "Sliding? Nina and Benny are cool with each other, but not cool like that."

India said, "Gloria claims they were getting in a cab together the night before last."

"You know Gloria is such a fucking liar, so I don't know if you should believe that shit."

"All I know," India said, "Is I have not seen Benny or my motherfucking paycheck in two fucking days. I knew if somebody knew where Nina was at, that someone would have been you."

Now I was sitting there in total disbelief. I said, "Oh my God Indy, I'm sorry about your check, but I have not seen Nina in three weeks. Girl, I filed a missing person's report two weeks ago, but I still have not heard anything back yet. I'm real worried about her."

India looked over at me like I was crazy, then she flipped the fuck out. "Fuck being worried, I'm mad as hell. That broke bitch Benny had the nerve to steal from me and my fucking daughter. After all I did for him, this is how he pays me back. That's alright, though, payback is a bitch, and we will see who has the last laugh."

Homegirl was so mad that she called Benny's parole officer, Mr. Sherman. She told him that Benny was missing in action and that was all she wrote. When Mr. Sherman caught up with Benny's ass, he would send Benny back to jail to finish off the rest of his time. India figured she was justified in what she did. Benny should not have stolen her money. When India calmed herself down, I told her what Linda and Stacey said to me about Nina, then India was the one in shock.

We were playing a game of racquetball, tossing information back and forth. Then she told me that Benny had been smoking crack for the last seven months. All I could think was, not super duper fly Benny. Gator-wearing, different-color-mink-having Benny who would not wear the same outfit twice. Now he was smoking crack. Drugs were taking the world by storm, and I was asking myself, is this what the world is coming to?

After hearing all that shit, you know we had to smoke a blunt to get our mind right. India had some good chocolate from dyckman in upper Manhattan. After four blunts of that good shit we were so high we could not even move. Shonda came home not long after that and cooked dinner, and after we ate we just sat around and reminisced about the good old days. A few hours later India went home, but before she left I asked her where Asia was, and she told me she was at her mother's house in Brooklyn.

India said that Asia would be back next week, and I told her to give her a kiss for me when she came home. I told India that if I heard anything about Benny or Nina I would let her know and she said she would do the same. After she was gone we were all tired, so we went to sleep. When I got up the next morning I started my search all over again, only this time I went to the Bronx. That's where we used to go with India to see Benny back in the day.

I knew some of Benny's friends from around this area—of course I *really* knew some of them. As I continued my search I ran into a few of them, and I got a few laughs for the day. The first dude I ran into was Shawn, aka Light. Light looked damn good. He's six foot two, two hundred and fifty pounds, solid, and he has some good dick, too. But Light was broker then broke—let me tell you what I mean by that statement. When I fucked him he gave me two thousand dollars for a round house.

A round house is sucking dick, licking ass, licking balls, toes and any other place that he wanted licked. Every hole can be penetrated with any object that the man desires. If you were with it, things could also get very freaky-deaky if you get my meaning. Yes, it was a few hours of being a ho in every sense of the word, but hey, somebody had to make that money, why not me?

After we were done handling our business, Light kept giving me drinks on top of drinks on top of more fucking drinks. When he felt I was drunk enough, he tried to take my motherfucking money back. The money was my fee for a job well-done and I would be damned if this high yellow bitch was going to play me. Now what type of shit was that? I started yelling and going crazy, throwing shit at him, and then I pulled out Mary. I was going to cut his fucking throat from ear to motherfucking ear for my money, but Light backed down and gave me my money back. That was the last time I saw his shady ass.

Now here he was, looking over at me smiling, then he had the nerve to say, "Jazmine, what's good, baby girl?" As if we were still friends.

So I yelled back, "Not your broke ass, now nigger keep it moving, and I kept on going. The next guy I ran into was La. Now La is a dime piece and he knew it. Five foot seven, dark chocolate, wavy hair, and a full goatee, he was fine as aged wine. But La did not want any pussy. He was willing to pay one thousand dollars just for you to lick his ass. So one night I finally gave in, and I got the saran wrap and went to work.

I licked his ass to the core of his soul, and after two hours of my powerful tongue I put his ass right to sleep. Not to long after that we found out that La was gay. Ruben, his roommate, was his undercover lover, but the only one under cover was La. One summer night that shit hit the fan, and it was not a pretty sight. Ruben came outside that night and put La on full blast. La had been fucking Ruben's cousin Hector for five months, and Ruben was pissed. Ruben over heard La tell Hector that he was leaving Ruben for him and they were going to become a couple.

Ruben was out there screaming and yelling, waving his hands in the air and snapping his fingers. You know how faggots do. That was the last time that I saw La until today. I was waving to La, trying to hold in a laugh, but he was acting like I wasn't even there. I knew he saw me, shit I was waving both my hands in the air, acting like an idiot. La was ignoring me and I got upset. Then I said to myself, it wasn't my fault that he was not a real man, and that's when I bumped right into Benny.

Benny was so damn high he did not even recognize me, so I yelled out, scaring the shit out of him, "Benny, where the hell is Nina, and where the fuck is India's money?"

Benny looked up at me like he had just seen a damn ghost. His lips were all white and chapped, and he was sweating like he had just run a marathon. He wiped his face off and then he started speaking, "Oh shit, Jazmine, I was just looking for you, where are you coming from?"

His lie pissed me off more then I already was, so I said, "Motherfucker, you know I don't live over here. So how the hell was you just looking for me?"

He started saying some dumb shit out of his month like, "Yeah, I know you don't live over here but I was on my way downtown to get you right now."

All I was thinking was this nigger has got to be crazy, and then I had a thought. No, Benny was not crazy. Benny was on crack, and I was disgusted to the point that I wanted to throw up. I said, "Shut up, stupid, and tell me where Nina is, and where is India's money?"

Benny said, "Okay, Jazmine, let me tell you what happened." He was taking so long to talk that I said, "Motherfucker, you better tell me what I just asked you, or I am going to kick your motherfucking ass."

"Alright, Jazz, listen, the other day my brother Miguel called me," then Benny stopped looked up at me, and asked me, "You know my brother, Miguel, right?" When I did not answer him he said, "Well, Miguel got locked up the other day and I took India's check to go and bail him out. When I left the building, I ran right into Nina at the corner store. After I told her what happened, she said that she would come with me to bail Miguel out of jail. We took a cab up here to my mother's house so I could get Miguel a change of clothes, and when we got out the cab guess what happened, Jazz?"

By now my patience was wearing thin, so I said, "Benny, I don't care about any of these lies that you want me to believe. Just tell me what I asked you."

He interrupted me at that point and said, "Alright, Jazz, since you won't guess, I will tell you what happened. We got robbed."

I had to laugh. He couldn't come up with something more creative then that? I said, "Alright, Benny, that explains the money part, but where the hell is Nina?"

He started stuttering, "Well, you see when we got robbed, Nina got scared and took off running." He pointed up the street and said, "She went that way, and I have not seen her since."

I tried to keep my voice calm. I asked Benny one more time, "Where the hell is Nina? You better stop all this motherfucking lying and tell me the goddamn truth, Benny. And just for the record, I know that you have been smoking crack for the last seven months. So once and for all, tell me where the fuck Nina is, or I will have to hurt you."

At that point I pulled out Mary, my trusted scalpel. I said, "Benny, you have gotten on my last nerve, and if you don't stop playing with me I will slice your fucking throat from ear to ear. Nigger, I mean I will split you wide-the-fuck open."

Benny's eyes opened wide, and they were moving real quick back and forth. He was probably wondering if I was dead serious or what, but I guess the look in my eyes said it all. So finally he started to tell me a different story, the true story.

"Look, Jazmine, I know I was wrong for stealing India's money, and I'm real sorry that I did it. But this monkey is on my back hard, and I can't seem to shake it."

"Benny, you could get help if you really wanted it. Now where the fuck is Nina?"

He looked down and said real low, "She's at my mother's house."

"Where is your mother, Benny?"

"She's in Puerto Rico. We were using her house while she's been gone."

"You mean to tell me that you and Nina have been hiding out over here all this time?"

Not looking me in my face, he said, "Yes, Jazmine, we have been here all this time."

All I could think was, *All this bullshit just so they can get high?* Then I said, "Shit, Benny, take me upstairs." He did not utter a sound the whole ride up on the elevator, and it was a very tense ride. When we got to the apartment, Benny unlocked the door, and then he turned and walked away looking all nervous and shit like a fiend would do. Then he said, "Please don't tell India that you saw me, alright?"

I was so mad at him; all I could say was, "Yeah, whatever Benny. Just get your life together. You have a wonderful child to see grow up, and a beautiful women who loves you more then life itself.

"Do what you have to do to clean yourself up, and go on home to your family. Benny, life is too short, and you need help now." After I gave him those words of wisdom I turned away. Looking at Benny was making me sick to my stomach, and I wondered what I would find behind the closed door in front of me. I opened the door and the smell of crack hit me hard.

Before I could catch my breath, Nina started calling out Benny's name. She was asking if he had the crack, and as she got close she said, "Damn, what took you so fucking long? I was starting to think that you were never coming back."

Nina walked from the back of the house not paying attention, and then she saw me and froze. I yelled, "Bitch, you have me looking all over the damn place for you. Calling the police and shit, and your ass is up in here smoking fucking crack with Benny. Bitch I should beat the shit out of you." You would not believe what this bitch had the nerve to say.

"Jazmine, hey girl, I have been calling Shonda and Wella's house looking all over for you. I have even been calling your cell phone for days, and no one ever answers. Where the hell you been hiding?" All I heard was my fist hitting Nina's face, and her lying ass hitting the floor.

When she came to, I was standing over her looking evil as hell, and then I asked her, "So now you're smoking crack again?"

She cried out to me, "No, Jazmine, I am not smoking crack."

"So now you're a full-fledged crackhead?"

She cried out, "No, Jazmine!"

"Nina, look at me. Bitch, you fucking dogs and God knows what else, so these little drug dealing bastards can give you a fix?"

She looked up and said, "Jazmine, whoever told you that bullshit is lying."

"Nina, I can see it all in your face, so stop lying to me. You know that you can get some help. You know that you can beat this addiction. You did it before." By now Nina was crying uncontrollably.

She cried out, "Get help for what? I have AIDS, remember. I'm going to die anyway, Jazz."

"Nina, your life is not over. If you get help now this can be just the beginning."

She cut me off in mid sentence and said, "No Jazz, you're wrong my life is over, and all these motherfuckers out here who want to fuck me will fuck me. If I have to die, I might as well take as many of those stupid-ass bastards that I can with me."

I was stunned. I said, "Nina, you can't do that, it's just not right."

She screamed, "I can do it and I will do it. I can do anything that I want to do, fuck doing what's right all the time. Jazmine, what the fuck has anyone ever done for me, what has ever gone right in my life? My fucking father is my mother's perverted-ass uncle who raped her. My mother could not handle life, so she left me with my grandparents who died before my sixth birthday. Then there was the joke of a foster care system.

"They were supposed to look out for me, until I was old enough to look out for myself. Look what happened, Jazz, they failed me. My mother died from AIDS at thirty-four and left me all alone, and I have no one in this world but you. Now I have HIV and I'm going to die the same way that my mother did. No one loves me but you, and soon you will go back to Mink, then who will I have? Nobody."

"Nina, I will never leave you, it's you and me against the world. You know that. But you have to want to live." I was holding her, crying, telling her that I needed her to live. "Please, Sis, live for me, you know Shonda and little Ty love you and we all need you." I don't know how long we sat in the dark side by side, and when my phone rang it was Mink. I answered the phone and told him that everything was fine. I told him Nina and I were getting something to eat at Copeland's on 145th Street, and when we were finished I would call him back.

Nina and I left Benny's house at eleven that night and took a cab straight to the projects. We went to Wella's house because Nina said that she did not want Shonda and little Ty to see her looking so bad. For the first time that day, I noticed how bad Nina really looked. She had on some filthy clothes that weren't even her size. Her hair was matted to her head, and she was beyond stink. I looked up to God and prayed, Lord please help my sister, for she knows not what she does.

A little while later Nina took a bath, ate a tuna fish sandwich, and laid down. She kept repeating over and over again, "Jazz, I am so tired." I don't know how many times she repeated that statement before she finally drifted off to sleep. But sleep was something that did not come easily for me that night. I knew that soon Nina would have to unload her confessions, and I wanted to be prepared to hear her out. It was five in the morning before I forced myself to go sleep, and all I was thinking of was the drama and heartache, and when would it all end?

Chapter Eight

Confusion

Three weeks had passed. Nina and I stayed in the house the entire time doing absolutely nothing. We talked, ate, and slept, and the only people I spoke to were Shonda and Mink. My daddy made sure the money kept coming in. Every three days Shonda was at Western Union, collecting that paper. The money was good, but damn a bitch needed some tender loving care, and a whole lot of dick.

Mink had been in Virginia for close to eight months now on a mean paper chase. Even though I spoke to him two times a day, it was hard, because he had not been home once in all that time. I know he was getting some pussy from somebody, so if he was fucking one of those country bitches I hoped that he was using a condom. Oh well, I had too much other shit on my mind to drive myself crazy worrying about what he was doing. As long as he took care of home, he could have all the fun that he wanted with those chicken heads.

Every time I spoke to him I told him to wrap it up if he was cheating on me. Because what you do in the dark will eventually come to the light. Every time I told him that, he would always say the same thing, "Jazz, you are tripping, I am not having sex with any of these females down here. I only want you and your pink kitty cat."

Yeah right I knew that if I was not sleeping with him, somebody sure in hell was. Now I loved money, but I loved my man more and I wanted him to come home. There are only three fates in the drug game. You make it out alive, you go to jail, or you die. I knew that Mink wanted to be sitting on millions when he retired, so all I could do was pray that everything worked out for the best. Every day I asked God to watch over him and let him make it out in one piece. All he seemed to care about were those dollar signs. Money came before everything else in his life, and as much as it hurts me to admit it, money came before me.

I was talking to my girl the other day, and Nina said that she wanted to get clean and sober. She did not want to go into an inpatient program, but she would do an outpatient one. I told her if that's what she wanted to do then I was fine with that. At least now we had a game plan to focus on. We decided that we would stay in the house for the next couple of weeks until she was ready to make a move.

Nina wanted to gain a little weight first, and then she would sign into Daytop. It was a well-known drug treatment program in lower Manhattan. It had good results for addicts who wanted to get their lives back on track. Shonda did the grocery shopping for us every week so I didn't have to leave Nina alone in the house. It was such a quiet and peaceful time for us—it was very relaxing and just what we needed.

Nina talked about a lot of the things that had been bothering her. She talked about the rape of her mother and her own rape that would prevent her from ever having children in the future. She also talked about having the same disease that took her mother away from her. Nina needed a shoulder to lean on, a sounding board, so all I did was listen. We cried a lot, and laughed even more.

Even though Nina had a whole lot of problems in her life, homegirl was still silly as hell, and it was nice to hear her laugh. Then I talked to Mink, and he said that he was coming home for a few days so I better get ready. I arranged for Nina to baby-sit little Ty over the weekend so Shonda and Michael could have some adult time, I think its been awhile for them both. Now that every base was covered, I was going to do all the things that adults like to do. When Friday finally arrived I was thirsty as hell to see my man, and I was ready to go.

I got my hair done at Clara's on 112th Street and Fifth Avenue, and then I went to Uptown Nails on 125th Street and Seventh Avenue to get my nails done. When I walked out of that place I felt fierce. Then I went to Pathmark for groceries, because I was going to make a meal fit for a king. We were going to have Mink's all-time favorite meal—T-bone steak, jumbo shrimp, and baked macaroni and cheese. Of course we needed something to drink. I got Hennessy for Mink and Absolute Vodka for me.

I already knew what I was going to put on to seduce my man. I pulled out my red mink negligee, and my red mink feathered slip-on sandals. I prepared our meal as soon as I got in the house, then I took a nice hot bubble bath with my vanilla body oils, another one of Mink's favorites. When my bath was complete, I dimmed all the lights in the house, lit some candles, and then I went to our stereo system to find some music. I put on a seduction CD that had all the best slow jams on it. It was just right for making love. Then I just sat back and chilled until my man came home.

Mink got in about six that evening. I heard the keys jingling in the door, and when he pushed the door open, I was standing there like a dog in heat waiting for my dick to come and claim its pussy. He came in, dropped his bag on the floor, grabbed me, and pulled me toward him. He kissed me real deep, that kiss said that he really missed me, and he was happy to be home. He turned me over to face the wall, all the time feeling all over my breasts and ass.

Then he bent me over, pulled up my gown and gave me all thirteen inches of his dick. I screamed out, "Yes, Daddy, fuck me, oh Daddy, yes fuck me harder. Daddy, I've missed you so much, harder, Daddy, harder." The whole time that I was screaming and moaning, Mink was banging my pussy like he would never feel it again, and I gave it all to him. We did every position imaginable, and then some more that we made up as we went farther along.

My love nest was raw by the time we were done, but it was all good because that was just what I needed, Mink's big black stiff dick. At ten o'clock we finally stopped. We jumped in the shower but could not contain ourselves, so we made love for one more hour. At eleven fifteen we finally sat down to eat, and when Mink and I walked into the kitchen and he saw the feast that I had prepared he was shocked.

"Damn, baby girl, this shit here is beautiful, you must have really missed a nigger, huh?" Then he pulled me to him, and kissed me on both of my cheeks, and then he slapped my ass real hard. After all the kisses, and before he got aroused again, I thanked him for the compliment, and told him to have a seat. Damn, it felt real good to be appreciated. We sat down to a quiet candlelit dinner for two. Throughout the meal we talked, catching up on what had been going on in each of our lives. Even though we talked every day, there were still a few things we may have forgotten to tell one another.

I asked him if Tyrell had come up with him from Virginia.

He looked at me real strange, and said nothing, and then he shook his head and said, "No, that nigger said he don't have a girl in New York, so why come up here? He said that he was going to stay down there, and get all the paper that I was going to miss by coming home to see you." I was looking at him with a disgusted expression on my face, and then he said, "Baby girl don't look like that, I stopped Tyrell dead in his tracks. I told him that whatever money I missed, you were well worth it."

I smiled at Mink, and said, "That was a good idea, Daddy. Let him hold down the fort until you get back."

I was so glad that bastard Tyrell did not come with him. If he had, he would have been all up under Mink's ass, and that would not have been acceptable to me. We talked a little bit about Nina, and then I told him about Shonda's new man, Michael. I told him little Ty was doing okay, and after we talked for another hour we cleared the table together.

We made love one more time that night, and then sleep took over our souls. We were asleep in a matter of seconds, until the sun woke us up the next morning. The next two days were the best days that I have had in a long time. On Saturday morning my man brought me breakfast in bed. We had scrambled eggs, bacon, grits, orange juice, and toast with butter and jelly. Tea for me and coffee for Mink, and on the tray were pink rose petals sprinkled around my food. It was so beautiful. We fed each other and a peaceful calm settled over me. After that big breakfast we lounged around watching television and chilled out for the rest of the day.

On Sunday afternoon, Mink said that he wanted to go outside and get something to eat. Since we had been in the house ever since he got into town, we needed some fresh air. We went to Jezebel's one of our favorite restaurants in downtown Manhattan. Mink had the seafood combination and I had the lobster and shrimp special. We shared a bottle of white wine that was chilled to perfection, and had a beautiful night.

We talked about anything and everything. We were two people in love. After we finished the first bottle of wine, my daddy ordered another bottle, only this time he ordered red. When the waiter left with our order, Mink looked over at me and winked his left eye, and then he said we were going to mix things up a little bit. People don't know this, but wine will get you drunk as hell. It will fuck you up, take my word for it.

As the night wore on we got drunker and drunker. Mink said that he had something that he needed to say to me, so I gave him my undivided attention.

He said, "Jazmine, I have been doing some serious thinking these past few months, and I have made a decision. I love you with all my heart, and with all this money that I am making it only brings trouble. All I see out here are money hungry bitches. They make me realize what a real women you are, and how bad I need you in my life forever."

I looked up, and asked him, "Forever, Mink?"

He smiled and said, "Yes baby girl, forever." Then he got down on one knee. With tears in his eyes he asked, "Jazmine Marie Roberts, will you marry me?" He was holding the biggest eight-carat marquise center cut diamond ring I had ever seen.

I screamed, "Oh my God, Mink, it's beautiful. It's the biggest ring I have ever seen in my life."

Mink was laughing, and then he asked the million-dollar question again. "Jazmine Marie Roberts, will you marry me?"

I looked at him like he was crazy and said, "Will I marry you? Hell yes I will marry you for this big ass ring! Shit, I will marry ten of you for a ring like this." I did not realize I was that loud until everyone in the restaurant started clapping. They were all saying congratulations, and it was the happiest day of my entire life. That night we made passionate love and fell asleep in each other's arms.

Monday morning he finally had to leave, but it was all good because we were engaged now. Mink told me that he would try to come back home over the weekend, and that he loved me. He gave me three thousand dollars, and told me to tell Nina to stay strong and keep her head up. Mink did not know that Nina had the HIV virus, and I felt that it was not my place to tell him Nina's business. He felt like Nina should take the losses in her life and just keep on moving, but it was not that easy. When every day you open your eyes and you know that you are closer and closer to your death, life can become real unbearable.

I could not wait to get uptown to tell Nina and Shonda that I was getting married. I knew that they both would be happy for me, but what mattered most was that I was happy. When I got uptown Nina was the only one in the house, she was sitting on the couch watching television and eating a bowl of cereal. I was going to wait until Nina noticed my ring, but my expression must have said it all. She looked at my face, and then she looked at my ring finger and started screaming.

"Girl, look at that damn rock!" Homegirl was talking a mile a minute, and she was asking a million questions. Did you set a date yet? What colors do you want us to wear? Then she told me that I better tell her everything, and not leave a thing out. I told her all about my weekend, and then she said tomorrow she would go sign up for the drug program. I was very proud of her, because she wanted to be clean for my wedding.

When Shonda and little Ty came home, Nina had cooked dinner already, so all we had to do was eat. I told Shonda about my engagement to Mink, and then I showed her my extra-big ring. Girlfriend was overjoyed, and after she calmed down we talked about when the wedding should be, what colors we should wear, who would be invited, and the food. After we talked for two more hours, and with our bellies full from dinner, we all sat back and watched *Coming to America*. Eddie Murphy is a funny motherfucker, and we laughed until tears came out of our eyes.

The next morning we started out early. Nina and I had a light breakfast at the house, and then we got to Daytop at nine on the dot. The registration process was very long, but when everything was said and done she had been signed up for a six-day program for the next six months. We hoped by then the urge to use drugs would be gone, and my sister would be back to her old carefree self, minus her addiction.

Mink and I set a date for the wedding. It would be on August the sixth, which was my birthday. Nina and Shonda would be my bridesmaids, little Ty would be the ring bearer, and India's daughter, Asia, would be the flower girl. I spoke to Mink's parents and they were both happy for us. Miracle said that she wanted to be a junior bridesmaid so everything was all set. We decided that my wedding gown would be pearl and white satin. I would have a long train and a diamond tiara with a veil. The bridesmaid dresses would be pearl, like a soft silver to match the groomsmen's suits, which will be white with a silver cummerbund. I could not wait.

We were going to be married in a small ceremony in Central Park at night by the waterfall. An old family friend of the Greens who was an ordained minister would perform the service, so everything was almost in place. The reception would be held at Mars 2112 in Manhattan, invite only. I was so excited that I thought I was going to burst. It was a really good feeling.

On another good note Nina and I received our GED results, and just like I thought we passed with flying colors. We were both looking forward to moving on with our lives, her drug-free and my white ass married. If a man tried to pick me up I would say, "I's married now," just like Sug Avery said in *The Color Purple.* All of a sudden Mink had been coming home every weekend ever since we got engaged. He said it was to give me some much-needed attention, but he was the one who needed all the attention. That was okay with me because I loved my man, and my life was finally on the right track

I was on cloud nine, preparing for my upcoming wedding to the most perfect man in the world. Nothing could take away my joy. It was hard to believe that five months had passed, and Nina had been in the program without one incident. She seemed to be doing well, when out of nowhere she became very quiet and withdrawn once again. No laughing, smiling, joking, no nothing. She was hardly eating any food, and started to lose weight. For the life of me, I could not figure out what was wrong with her. A few days later all my questions were answered.

Nina's counselor, Mrs. Sheldon, gave me a call. She said that she had to see me immediately, it was of great importance. I asked her if Nina was all right, and she said she was not and that it was very important that we spoke right away. I told her that I would be there shortly. The whole ride downtown I was very nervous and anxious, and I knew that once again my friend had slipped. When I got to the drug program I let the front desk know that I was there. The receptionist let Mrs. Sheldon know that I had arrived, and then she showed me right into her office.

When I walked in I saw that Nina was sitting there on the couch with her eyes swollen from crying. She looked sick, and afraid. I said, "Nina, what's the matter?" She wouldn't turn her head to look at me.

Mrs. Sheldon walked over to me, shook my hand, and then said, "Jazmine, Nina has started using drugs again. She has relapsed, and she was scared to tell you, so I told her that I would tell you for her. Nina said that she still wants to continue her rehabilitation, so we are going to send her to our inpatient program upstate. It is a twenty-four month program, and it will only work if she wants it to. She will be leaving sometime this evening. You can bring her some clothes she will need for the trip, but nothing else.

"She does not need any money, maybe just a few books and crossword puzzles. Whatever you think that she will like, but all she needs is a change of scenery and a lot of rest. She feels that if she stays here in the city, then she will never get clean. Maybe going to the country will give her a sense of peace that she can't find here. Now I'll leave you two alone so you can talk in private."

When Mrs. Sheldon left the room I didn't know what to say to Nina, so I said nothing at first, and then I started telling Nina I knew she was still weak, but she had to be strong.

Nina finally looked over at me and said, "Jazz, I'm sorry. Please don't be mad at me. I don't know what happened."

"So that's why you were so quiet. Nina, why didn't you talk to me? Why did you start using drugs again? Nina, talk to me."

She looked down at the floor, and then she looked back up at me with eyes so sad all I could do was take a deep breath to stop myself from crying. I took a seat next to her to get my thoughts together, and that's when Nina started talking.

She told me some chick from the program named Janine offered the drugs to her. Nina said they became fast friends the first week she came to Daytop. Janine also had AIDS, and she told Nina that she understood what she was going through because she lived with it herself every day. Janine had been in four treatment centers, and she always relapsed. Taking someone down with her was nothing, Nina was just her latest victim. Nina said Janine knew that she was still weak, and that the temptation was very strong. Janine not only tempted Nina with the drugs, but she also took three other females from the program down.

After that talk with Nina, I went back uptown to Wella's house and packed Nina a bag of clothes to take with her. I also sent her three books that I thought she would like, shit everybody loves a good story. I sent her The Coldest Winter Ever By Sister Souljah, Situations by Queen Pen, and True To The Game by Teri Woods. Now I was ready to take the trip back downtown to deal with all this confusion, and to see my sister off on her road to self discovery.

When I got to Daytop, the bus had just arrived to take Nina upstate. I gave my sister a hug and a kiss, and told her to call me as soon as she could. So many emotions were running through my mind, I just needed some time to myself. I took the train and went downtown to 42nd Street and Seventh Avenue, and then I walked to the wax museum. Once I purchased my ticket and was shown inside I just walked around and around. I was not really looking at the displays. I was just thinking, trying to clear my head. After I did that for a few hours, I went across the street to the Olive Garden for a quiet Italian dinner. I was beyond starving, and I felt like I was about to fall the fuck out. After that I went home and lay my tired ass down and was fast asleep in the blink of an eye.

Chapter Nine

Deception

A few days after Nina left for the program, Shonda called and asked me where Nina was. She had not seen her in a few weeks. I forgot that I had not spoken to my sister in awhile, so I told her everything that had happened in the last few days. She listened quietly, and then she said maybe it was all for the best that Nina went away. She told me not to worry, and that everything would be fine in no time. We talked for a little while longer, and then I told her that I would see her and little Ty over the weekend. I told her to give my little man a kiss for me and then we hung up.

I had felt nauseous all morning. I ate some crackers and drunk some ginger ale, hoping the feeling would pass. But it did not, and all I had the strength to do was put the garbage can by my bed and lay my sick ass down. Mink called me at seven that evening saying that he missed me, and he just wanted to hear my sweet and sexy voice. We spoke for a little while longer, and then Mink said that he would be home in a few days. He told me to get his pink kitty cat ready, and then ten minutes later we hung up and a second later I was asleep.

The next morning, all I could do was bend over and let the garbage can catch all my vomit. I threw up nonstop for twenty minutes, twenty whole minutes. After that there was nothing left but a dry heave, I was a mess. I pulled myself together about 2pm that afternoon, and I went to see my doctor. She confirmed what I already knew, I was three months pregnant. She told me to keep eating the crackers, and since I was in my first trimester, my upset stomach would soon pass. I had a sonogram and got my prenatal vitamins, but I was too sick to be happy. When I got home I called Mink and told him the good news. He was very happy, and after we talked for a little while longer I went back to bed.

The next month and a half I was a complete mess. The baby was kicking my ass. I finally got in the spirit, though, after I told Shonda the good news. Homegirl went crazy buying all kinds of shit, and Mink was just as bad as her. He gave me a hundred thousand dollars, and told me to open up a bank account for our unborn child's college education. I was beyond happy, and glad that my morning sickness had finally passed.

Everything was going well with the baby, and we still had a few more months before the wedding. Everything was almost in place. I have not heard from Nina yet, but I was not worried. Mrs. Sheldon told me that if Nina felt that she was not strong enough, then she would not be able to call home. So all I could do was pray, and hope that everything worked out for the best. Time was really flying, and I was starting to show. I was glowing—yes, being pregnant looked damn good on me. Everyone said so and I must agree with them.

Mink was home for a few days, and besides us being laid up every day all day, all we did was eat, sleep, and make love. Mink spent over ten thousand dollars on our unborn child, and he kept saying the same thing over and over again, "My baby is going to have everything I had as a child and more."

On Mink's third day home his mother called and invited us over for a few days. So we packed some clothes, and we went to spend a few days with his family at their great big house.

Mama Green pampered me from the time that we arrived. She was running around cooking all types of meals for me. And I ate everything she cooked, and after three hours I had eaten so much I was stuffed and tired. Pop treated me just like a queen. Miracle wouldn't leave me alone the whole time we were there, just rubbing my stomach and showing me mad love. I felt so relaxed, and it felt good not to have to worry about anyone or anything for a few days. Even though Nina was heavily on my mind, I managed to put my concerns to the side and just enjoyed being loved.

We came home the next week, and I discovered that Shonda had left several messages. Each message said the same thing. She said we had some trouble in the family, and for me to give her a call as soon as I got the messages. I hoped it was not anything too bad, but on the machine she sounded very upset. When I called Shonda's house little Ty answered the telephone, after we talked for a minute I asked him to put his mother on the phone. He put me on hold for a minute, and went to get his mom. When Shonda came on the line, she said hello, then she asked me about my time at the Green's. After I told her about my time away from home, she gave me some shocking news.

"Nina popped up at my house three days ago."

"I thought she was still in the program upstate?" I said.

"Nina left the program over a week ago. She told me she left because she could not handle all the pressure."

I asked Shonda, "How did Nina look?"

"She did not look good. She looked high, and she was acting real jittery. I let Nina stay because she said she was going to enter another program to get help. She told me she was real tired, and she just wanted to lay down for a few hours, but when she left the next morning so did little Ty's chain."

I was shocked at Nina's actions, but Shonda was just pissed off about little Ty's missing chain. Shonda said that she just wanted Nina to get some help, and to get her life back on track. It got very quiet on the line. I must have zoned out or something, because out of nowhere I heard Shonda yelling my name, asking if was I alright.

I said, "Yes, Shonda, I'm fine, I just can't believe what you just told me. I told her that if I heard from Nina that I would call her, but we both knew that the chain was history. If an addict had something to sell that shit would be gone in a matter of seconds. Shit, Nina probably sold it before she was even out of the building. I told Shonda that I loved her, and that I would keep her posted. All I could do was wait for Nina to call asking for help, and wait is what I did. I was very depressed over the next two days. Even though Mink was trying to be supportive, nothing he did was working.

The clock was ticking, and even though Mink did not want to leave me alone, he had no choice because money had to be made. I was sad to see him go, but I knew that it had to happen if we were going to survive. He stayed as long as he could, but two days later my soul mate had to leave me and my unborn child again. I prayed that night, and asked God to forgive me for my sins. I asked him to watch over Nina while she was out there on her mission, and to watch over Mink while he did his dirt.

I must have fallen asleep, because it was three thirty in the morning when my house phone rang. I knew it was Nina even before I picked up the telephone.

When I said hello all I heard was a low voice that said, "Please come and get me." "Where are you?" I asked. .

She said, "I'm on 139th Street and Lenox Avenue."

I told her that I would be there soon, and for her not to move from that spot. When the cab pulled up I looked out the window, and I almost did not recognize her. Damn Nina looked fucked up. She had not looked this bad since I found her with Benny in the Bronx awhile back. She was real dirty, and her hair looked liked a mess. Her clothes were two sizes to big, and all ripped up, and she had two black eye and a busted lip. When she got in the cab I asked her what happened, and who beat her up like that?

Nina looked at me and said, "Some motherfucker named Dee."

"Who the hell is Dee," I asked, "and where the hell do you know him from?" "From 115th Street and Second Avenue. He wanted my drugs and my pussy so I gave both of them to him. When we were done I laughed in his face and told him, I have HIV motherfucker and now so do you. That's when he got mad and started beating on me. When he was finished and left the room I got dressed and called you."

I was sitting there stunned, and all I could think to say was, "Damn, Nina." We didn't talk for the rest of the ride to my house in Queens. When we reached my house I gave Nina a towel and rag and told her to go take a bath. I made her something to eat, and when she was done in the bathroom she ate a little bit of soup and then we went to sleep. The next few days were hard for Nina, because she was a junkie and getting clean was not going to come quickly.

She went through withdrawal hard, and she had the shakes and was always real cold. Whenever she tried to eat something all she did was throw it back up, so food was not a priority to her right now. It was a real slow process, and we needed God more than ever right now. Slowly but surely Nina was trying to get her life back together, and before long a month had passed us by. Mink was still in Virginia collecting that paper, and once again he had not been home in a while. But every three days like clockwork he would call and tell me to go and pick up the money he had sent me. When he called home we only spoke for a minute, because he knew I was dealing with my girl and her shit.

It was a Saturday when Nina said she wanted to go outside and get some fresh air, so we took a nice long walk around my neighborhood. It was a beautiful clear and sunny day, and it just felt good to be alive. Nina said that the fresh air felt wonderful on her body, so we stayed out for a while, and just enjoyed the breeze. We sat in the park talking and just enjoying life. We watched the children play on the slide and the monkey bars.

When we got back to the house Nina said that she wanted to call Shonda. She wanted to apologize to her about disrespecting her and her home, and for stealing little Ty's chain. Shonda knew Nina had resurfaced, and that she was staying at my house. I had called Shonda the morning after I picked Nina up, and I let her know that she was safe. Shonda was glad that I had found her and that she was okay. She was still pissed off about everything that went down that day, but she said that when the time was right that they would talk, so I left it at that.

When Nina dialed her number I heard Shonda pick up on the second ring, so I left the room so they could talk in private. Twenty minutes later Nina came out of the room teary-eyed and upset. She said that Shonda let her have it. Shonda cursed her out. She just could not believe that Nina had stolen from her, and she did not like the deception. I knew that Shonda was going to get into Nina's ass.

After Shonda calmed down she told her, "Nina, if I did not care about you or your well-being, I would not have anything to say to you at all. We are a family, and family always has each other's back." Shonda also said that Nina needed to get her life together, not for us but for herself.

After their talk, Nina said that her heart felt much lighter. She said that she was going to give sobriety another try. She also asked me if I could give her a loan so that she could replace little Ty's chain. I told her I would give her the money, and I said that it was a gift from me to her. The next morning we went to Zales to buy a nice substitute. It was not the one that she stole from my nephew, but it would do just fine. After we purchased the replacement chain, we took the train straight uptown to Shonda's house.

Shonda was still at work, so Nina left the gift on her pillow with a note once again apologizing for her actions. When we left Shonda's house, we went to check on Wella's apartment because we had not been there in a while. Everything was still in order, so we decided to go back to my house to chill. When we reached the lobby, we bumped right into Benny and India. They both said hello, then India said that she would call me later so that we could talk in private.

Benny did not even look our way after he said hello. He refused to make eye contact with us at all. I also noticed that Benny had a duffel bag in his hands. I could not wait for Indy to call me so I could get the scoop on what was going on with them. As we walked through the front door, Stacey and Linda were in front of the building just looking real nasty. They were standing there doing absolutely nothing, just sucking up air with their ugly selves.

When we walked passed by them I swore that I heard Linda mumble something like, "There were two sluts sitting in a tree, sucking every man's dick that they could meet." But before I could turn around and react, Nina had punched Linda in her face.

Linda hit the wall hard and fell to the ground. Then that punk bitch Stacey started copping a plea, saying, "I don't want no problems with you'll, you got it." Nina and I laughed at them and just kept on walking. When we got to my place, Mink had left me a message on the answering machine. He said that he could not wait until I was Mrs. Jonathon Mink Green, and that he loved me very much. That message made me feel so good. It felt so good to be loved.

Nina and I were both hungry, so we ordered a pizza with everything on it and just relaxed. We both dozed off on the couch, and woke up the next morning to a ringing telephone. When I answered it, it was Shonda asking to speak to Nina. I passed her the telephone and went to the bathroom to wash up. After her conversation, Nina came out the room and gave me a hug, thanked me, and told me she loved me. The telephone rang a second time, and when I answered it was India.

She asked me how was I doing, and how was Nina doing with her addiction? I told her that she was living, just taking it one day at a time, and India said so was Benny. She said he had come around three weeks ago apologizing and begging to come back home.

She said, "You know how love makes you do crazy things? So of course I listened to my heart and took his ass back. When I saw you yesterday Benny was going to a twenty-four month program upstate to kick his habit."

Benny told her that he loved her and their child, and he would do anything in his power to make things right again.

I told her that I was happy for her, and that I hoped everything worked out for the best. She told me she hoped so too, I told her to give Asia a kiss for me. Then we hung up.

I felt guilty because I had never asked Nina if she had slept with Benny, knowing she had that disease that was going to kill her. I loved Nina, but I also had love for India and her child. India had a daughter to care for, and I did not want her to die because Benny was an addict.

I called out and asked Nina to come into the living room. When she sat down I just threw the question at her. "Nina, did you and Benny have intercourse when you were together? And please don't lie to me."

She looked at me with tears in her eyes, and said, "No, Jazmine, I would never do that. I could not take India away from Asia, knowing how bad I want children myself." Then Nina just cried. I sat there and said nothing, but in my heart of hearts I knew that Nina was telling me the truth. So that was the end of that conversation, and we would never need to have it again.

We really did not do much, in the days that followed our talk. All we did was eat, sleep, and talk shit. It felt good not to have to worry about anything or have any concerns. Mink and Tyrell came into town for the weekend, and I was so happy that I could not contain myself. They said that they wanted to hang out, so we went to Jimmy's Café in the Bronx for some seafood, and then to a little spot called P J's in Harlem. We danced all night and had a few drinks; of course because of my condition I was only able to have cranberry juice.

When we got back to the house we were all dead tired, so we just crashed and called it a night. The next day we got up, and after we situated ourselves, we went shopping at Macy's. Then we had a late lunch at my favorite fast food restaurant, Wendy's, and then we returned home to get ready for the night ahead of us. Tonight was very special for us because we were going to the Hustler's Ball.

The Hustler's Ball comes around every two years, and it was only for the biggest hustlers around the world. The real money-getters. It was invite only, and half of the people who were invited did not know who was giving it, they just knew that they got an invitation to attend. So you know my Mink and his man Tyrell were getting some serious paper.

When we got to the party, we were two of the best-dressed couples in the building, and believe me people had on some real fly shit.

We saw furs in different colors, there was short ones and long ones, and we saw chinchillas, foxes, and minks. Mink and I had on matching his and hers white chinchillas, and underneath his coat, Mink was wearing a custom-made white silk Armani suit. He had a powder pink rose in his breast pocket, powder pink and white gators on his feet, and a white and pink derby. He looked so damn good, like a dark chocolate kiss, that I wanted to eat him up right then and there.

I had on a white silk Armani maternity dress with pink and white gator loafers. Nina and Tyrell were also dressed to impress. They had on midnight blue mink coats with the matching hats. Underneath their coats they had on black Armani outfits. Nina had on a long sleeved seductive black mini dress, showing off her long, sexy legs. Tyrell had on a jet black suit with midnight blue trim that was made to fit his body alone, and I must say homeboy did look tasty.

When they had mentioned to us that we were going to the ball, I told Mink that Nina and I did not have anything to wear. Then he surprised me by pulling the outfits out of his garment bag, I was so surprised all I could do was hug my daddy and cry.

The party was on an island, so once we got down to Chelsea Piers a yacht took us across to the island. The name fit the island perfectly—it was called Paradise and I was in heaven.

We partied all night long and well into the morning. The yacht brought us back to the pier, and in the cab on our way home Tyrell said that we should stop and get breakfast. Mink asked the driver to take us to Midnight Express, a twenty-four hour diner. After we ate we were all tired, and we could not wait to get inside the house to crash. When we got back to the house, Mink and I said goodnight immediately and we left Nina and Tyrell in the living room to fend for themselves.

We slept until it was evening, and when we got up I was starving, and so was my unborn child. Neither one of us could go another minute without some food. I made a man's meal. We had steak with potatoes, white rice, and string beans. We all had plenty to eat, everyone except Nina. She was very quiet through out the entire meal, and I just thought that it was because she did not get enough sleep. So I left well enough alone. Now I know I should have questioned her. After we finished dinner Mink and Tyrell left to go back and make that money. So once again it was just my unborn child, Nina, and lonely me.

A little while later we were just relaxing and watching television when Nina said that she needed to talk to me about something important. She said when Mink and I went to bed, Tyrell kept asking her to have sex with him for old times' sake. She was crying by now, and I did not like where this story was going.

Nina said, "Jazmine, I told him no, but he would not listen. Then he punched me in my stomach, threw me on the couch, and took it from me. Jazmine, Tyrell raped me."

I just held her while she cried, and I could not wait to speak to Mink and tell him about his fucked-up friend.

Nina just kept crying, and then she asked me, "Jazz, why is my life so fucked up? I have been raped twice, I am HIV positive, and soon I'm going to die." As I was sitting there holding her, it hit me. Oh my God, Tyrell may have been infected with the HIV virus. When I told Nina what I was thinking she said, "Oh well, that motherfucker should have left me the fuck alone. I did tell him no, and no does mean no, right, Jazmine?"

I just looked at her, because there was nothing for me to say to her. It seemed like our lives were constantly going around in circles, and none of it was for the good. We were both exhausted, so we both went straight to bed. A few hours later the telephone rang and woke me up from a deep sleep. When I answered the phone it was Mink, and he said that he just wanted to let me know that he had made it back down to the spot safe and sound.

I was a little bit disoriented, so I told him to hold on. I looked on the other side of the bed and there was no Nina. I looked on my nightstand, and my engagement ring was gone. I jumped out of the bed, and I ran into the living room to see if Nina was in there asleep, but Nina was nowhere to be found. She did not leave a note or anything. I picked up the living room phone and told Mink that I would call him back in twenty minutes.

After we hung up I tore my bedroom apart looking for my damn ring, but it was nowhere to be found. In my heart I already knew that Nina had taken it.

I yelled out, "Damn, why is something always going on in my life?" I wanted to lash out and hit someone, but there was no one around for me to attack. I called Mink back and told him that Nina had stolen my ring. Mink was pissed the fuck off. He was screaming and cursing, and the whole time we had been together I had never heard him this mad before. He was calling Nina all types of names, and then I told him about Tyrell beating and raping her, and then I told Mink that Nina was HIV positive.

After I said that Nina had the virus that causes AIDS, Mink got very quiet, and when he spoke again his voice was real low almost unrecognizable.

"Jazz, you mean to tell me that Nina has been sick all this time, and you did not tell me?"

I said, "Mink, Nina did not want anyone to know about her condition. She did not want people looking at her differently."

The line went dead for five minutes and then Mink said to me, "Jazz, let me call you back later on, okay?"

I said, "Alright, Boo, I love you."

And Mink said, "Yeah, Boo, I love you too." When we hung I had no idea that would be the last conversation that I would have with Mink for quite some time.

Chapter Ten

Love Lessons

A month had gone by with barely a word from Mink and no word at all from Nina. It seemed like Nina had fallen off the face of the earth again, and I had only spoken to Mink twice in all that time. When I did speak to him he told me that he was dealing with a lot of shit with Tyrell, and that I needed to give him some space. Mink said that Tyrell was really going through a lot right now, and he had to be there for his man. I understood that Tyrell was his man and all but I was his future wife, and I was carrying his child. Didn't that mean anything?

By now I was six and a half months pregnant big as a damn house, and I just felt incomplete. Shonda and little Ty came to check on me, and we had a ball, but I was still hurting inside about all the drama that was surrounding my life once again. On a more positive note, Shonda and Michael were doing great, and it seemed that her life was finally on the right track. I was very happy for her that she had a good man who loved her and her child. But I was very sad for myself, and I really needed a pick-me-up. On Sunday after Shonda and little man left Mama Green called and asked me to spend a few days with them out at their house, and that's just what I did.

Being at the Green's house was great. It was just what I needed and they treated me like a princess the whole time that I was there. They were feeding me anything and everything that they thought I needed to eat and I ate it all just like a fat pig. But when the week was up I was glad to be going home. When I got back home Mink had left me a message two days earlier telling me to go to money gram to pick up the five thousand dollars he had sent me. No I love you, no nothing—just go and get the money.

Then he hung up. I called his cell phone, and when I did not get an answer I called the number that he normally called me from.

Some guy picked up, and I asked him could I speak to Mink. He told me that Mink did not come around there anymore. I asked him was he sure, and he said yes, then he hung up on me. I was so worried, that I dug up Tyrell's cell phone number from out of Mink's old phone book. Tyrell's number was disconnected, so now I was really going crazy. I was wondering what the hell was going on. Did they get locked up or was it something much worse? After I prayed and calmed myself down enough to talk, I called the Green's house.

Pops answered on the second ring, and before he could get out a hello, I asked him if he had heard from his son. I told Pops that I had not spoken to Mink in a few days, and I was real worried that something bad had happened to him. Pop's told me that he spoke to Mink a little while after I left, and that he sounded fine. He told me to take it easy and for me not to worry. But I was six months pregnant—of course I was going to worry.

Three months had gone by and I was getting bigger and lonelier by the minute. There was still no word from Nina, and instead of Mink calling me he would call his brother Reggie, and have him call and tell me to go to money gram.

When I asked Reggie why Mink was not calling me himself, all he would say to me was, "Little Sis, don't worry yourself, you know Mink loves you and his baby more than life itself. Just take it easy and don't stress yourself out, just wait and give Mink a little more time to get his head on straight, and I promise you that everything will be all right real soon."

So I waited and I waited some more. My due date was getting really close and I was scared as hell. All I had was Shonda and the Greens, but at a time like this I needed Mink and Nina by my side. I prayed to God and asked him to please watch over me, and to send my man home to me soon. Two days before my due date my prayers were finally answered, and Mink magically reappeared. He walked in the living room, gave me a kiss on my forehead, and walked upstairs to the bedroom like everything was fine between us.

I was so angry that I had to take a deep breath to calm my damn nerves. When I walked into the bedroom, Mink was already fast asleep with all his damn clothes on. I just let the bastard lay there; I was so fucking mad that I was in a rage. That bastard had the nerve to come up in here, not say a damn word to me, and then just come in the room and go to sleep. Fine. If he did not have anything to say to me, then I wouldn't say anything to him either.

That very same night my contractions started. I felt like I had to go to the bathroom so I sat up in bed. I put my feet on the floor, stood up, and then my water broke. I went into the bathroom took a shower, and just waited. I did not want to say anything to Mink until the pain became too unbearable. By 5:00 AM I could not take it anymore, so I gave in. I started yelling and pushing on Mink. I told him to get his black ass up. I told him that my water had broke hours ago, and now it was time to go to the hospital for me to have his baby.

When he finally got up I was already dressed and I had my bags by the door. All I needed was a ride. When we reached Queen's General I was already nine centimeters dilated, and I could not wait to deliver this damn baby. Doctor Palmer told me that it would not be much longer, and he was right. Twenty minutes later, our daughter Mahogany Nicole Green arrived. She was born on April 11, 2000, and she was nine pounds and nine ounces. She was twenty inches long, and she had Mink's dark complexion with my hazel eyes. Mahogany was going to be a dime piece when she got older, and she was going to give her father fever.

Three days later I was released from the hospital, and the Greens picked us up. The ride home was very quiet, and Mahogany slept the whole time. When we got to my house, Mink had gone all out. There were balloons and flowers everywhere, and Mama Green had cooked a feast fit for a queen. It was enough food to last for days and I was so very hungry. I hated the hospital food, it wasn't seasoned so of course it had no taste. After I ate two plates of Mama Green's good soul food, I took Mahogany upstairs to put her in her crib. Even though she was a good baby, with all this company around, and everyone wanting to hold her she would be spoiled real quick.

Six months had passed and I still have not heard from my Nina. I prayed for her on a daily basis, but no one had seen or heard from her in months. Mink and I were on speaking terms, but not much more then that. No hugs, no kisses, and no sex. Mahogany was very fat, and she was growing faster by the day. Mink had been out of town a few times, but ever since I had the baby he was home much more. Him being home was not benefiting me at all, though, that bastard was not giving me any dick. I knew that he was cheating on me, but I had no real proof.

Whenever he came back home from out of town, I checked all of his pockets. I went through all his bags, and I even smelled his boxers. But I could not find any evidence or a scent that I could not recognize. I tried to talk to him about how I was feeling, and what I was going through, but he always pushed me away. Or he told me that I was bugging out, so I would just leave it alone. I wished Nina were around at a time like this. Shonda was here, and she would do anything for me, but Nina would have come up with a game plan, and she would have known exactly what I needed to do.

Diamond, as her father called her, was growing real fast, and she was already crawling and trying to walk. Mama Green said that the old folks always said that if a child started crawling, walking, or talking early, that meant that they were making room for another baby. In this case they were wrong, because Mink and I were not having any sex. We had not had sex since the baby was born, so I decided to take matters into my own hands. Diamond was going to stay with Shonda for the weekend, and the freak in me was about to come out.

I scattered rose petals all around the house, and made Mink's favorite meal. I was wearing my black see-through negligee, with the crotch cut out, and I had on my black feathered slip-on sandals. Now that I had everything set, the only thing missing was Mink. And you know what? That bastard never came home that weekend. He didn't even call. After I called his cell phone fifty fucking times I was so fucking angry all I could do was cry myself to sleep.

On Sunday I went to get my daughter, and when I got home Mink called and said that he was back from out of town. He was talking like everything was peaches and fucking cream, like everything was all good between us. I could not believe this nigger; he must have thought that I was a fucking fool or something. When I told him what I had planned for the weekend, he said that he was sorry that he missed it, and that he would make it up to me real soon. *Yeah right* I thought to myself, *how in the hell could he make this up?* I did not know what to do with myself; I couldn't just sit here and take Mink's bullshit so I did what I thought was best, I left the home that I shared with the man that I loved.

Instead of staying there to argue, when Mink finally decided to come home, I did the only thing that I could do. I packed up our things and Diamond and I moved back to Wella's apartment in Harlem. We had been gone for three whole weeks when Mink finally noticed that we were not at home with him. When he called my cell phone to find out where we were, I told him that we had moved out, and I told him that we were not coming back until he got his shit together. Of course he apologized and asked me to give him some more time.

I asked him, "How much time? Mink, I have given you my whole fucking life. I changed my whole damn lifestyle for you. So you know what, fuck you, Mink, you can take all the damn time that you need." I told him that I was done with his ass, and then I called him a black no-good bitch. I told him not to call me again, not until he was ready to be a man and take care of his family. After I hung up I cried for two whole days. This postpartum depression bullshit was really kicking my ass. All I really wanted to do was close my eyes and forget, and I was tired of all these love lessons. Shit, they were killing me softly.

The only good thing in my life right now was Diamond. I loved her so much it hurt. She was a very special baby and she was always happy, which was great for me. The weekend was rapidly approaching, and India said that she wanted to go out and party. Since I had nothing else to do, I told her that I was down to go. Shonda watched Diamond and Asia while India and I went out. We went to One Fish Two Fish on Ninety-seventh Street and Madison Avenue and had a great time.

After two hours of drinking Absolute and cranberry juice I was so drunk I could not stand up straight. I saw ghetto Stacey and ghetto Linda. Out of all the people for me to run into. These two bitches were everywhere. Linda saw me first and walked over. She said, "Hi, Jazmine, hi India. What's happening ladies?" India looked over and responded for the both of us.

"Hey girls, we're just chilling, what's up with you two?"

Stacey said, "Nothing, just trying to get our freak on."

India said, "I hear that."

"Jazz, I saw that fine ass man of yours," said Linda. "What's his name again, Mink, right?"

I looked at her and said, "Yes, that's his name, and you saw him where?"

She smirked, and said, "I saw him on 125th Street and Eighth Avenue the other day. He was with another fine ass dude, some light-skinned cat with curly hair."

After that I did not want to talk anymore, the conversation was over for me.

When they finally got the hint and walked off, I looked at India and said, "That bastard was up here in Harlem, and he did not come by to see his daughter. Wait until I get my fucking hands on him; right now I could kill him."

For the rest of the night I could not get my groove on like I wanted to, so all I did was drink. By 4:00 AM I was too drunk to stand up on my own, and India was not too far behind. The only difference between us was India was very happy, she ran into an old fling named Juice. She used to mess with him during high school, and from how they were carrying on, homegirl was going to get some dick tonight, and I was not mad at her

I finished my last drink for the night, and then I told India that I would see her on the block tomorrow, and then I got out of there. Instead of me going back to Saint Nick, I took a cab to my home in Queens. Something just kept telling me to go home. When I reached my house I put my key in the lock, and for some reason my heart was beating real fast. When I opened the door the whole house was in total darkness, but there were strange sounds coming from my bedroom upstairs.

When I got to my room, you would not believe what I saw. Mink was bent over on all fours while Tyrell was fucking him in the ass real hard.

I was in total shock, and I screamed out, "Mink, what the fuck is this, I know you're not fucking gay! And you brought this bitch in my house, nigger, in my fucking bed, oh hell no!"

Mink looked up when he heard my voice, and with fear in his eyes and said, "Jazz, I'm sorry, so sorry."

Then Tyrell looked back with a smirk on his face and said, "Hey, Jazz, you like what you see, do you want to join us?" All I could do was run to my hall closet and grab my .380 handgun.

I traded in my scalpel for a gun a while back, and my shit was always loaded with one in the fucking chamber. Everything seemed to be happening in slow motion, just like in the movies. Mink was rushing toward me, trying to grab the gun out of my hands, and I was shooting at anyone in sight. From the corner of my eye all I saw was that punk bitch Tyrell running past me.

He was running out of the room ass-naked, screaming, "This bitch is fucking crazy!" Mink and I wrestled on the floor for ten minutes, but I got the best of him. All I saw was the color red, and I don't even remember pulling the trigger. But when it was said and done I had shot Mink in his right shoulder, and he was bleeding quite profusely.

He managed to crawl to the house phone and dialed 911, but I was so upset with this homo bastard that I could not catch my fucking breath. I just kept saying the same thing over and over again, "In our home, in our fucking bed." Then it hit me. Oh my God, Mink was cheating on me, but with a man. And at that moment I wanted to kill him all over again, but where would that leave Diamond? I couldn't leave my precious daughter, so all I could do was ask Mink, "Why?" When the police came the front door was already open so they walked right in and came straight upstairs and right into the bedroom. Without asking what even happened they saw Mink bleeding, and they slapped the handcuffs on me and took me to jail.

I spent two days in jail before I saw a judge and was given bail. Shonda and Michael posted my bond, and got me out of there as fast as they could. They wanted me to come home with them, but I told them that I just needed to be alone for a while. They dropped me off in Queens, and the first thing that I did when I got in my house was call Mama Green to check on Diamond. She told me that my daughter was fine, and for me to take it easy. I thanked her, and then I asked her to give Diamond a kiss for me. When we hung up I looked around my house, and for the first time since I stepped inside I noticed that it was in shambles.

I wanted every trace of Mink gone, so it was time to clean house. I threw away everything that he owned, anything that was his was gone. I threw away his clothes, shoes, pictures, shaving cream, razors, and his cologne. Everything that belonged to that faggot had to go, and I could not get rid of his shit fast enough. In the bottom of Mink's closet I found a DVD marked, "Private, do not touch."

Now I was thinking what the fuck is this shit? So I put the DVD in, scared of what I might find. When it first came on, all I saw was darkness, but I heard all kinds of sexual sounds. Then as the picture came into view I saw several people having sex.

Not several different people, several different men to be exact. Mink, Tyrell, and four other sick motherfuckers were doing every position imaginable to mankind. The longer that I watched the filth I could not believe the shit that I was seeing. Mink sucked dick better then I did, shit probably better then you, too. His twisted ass was ridding Tyrell like he was in a rodeo trying to win a fucking medal.

This was some sick shit to see all these hard-ass niggers fucking, They were big diesel niggers, motherfucking thugs. They looked like they did nothing all day but lift fucking weights, but they were really giving up their ass, fucking butt bandits. They were fucking each other and they all seemed to be enjoying it, and they all had horse-sized dicks. I was sick to my fucking stomach; and all I could do was throw up over and over again for the next few hours.

Time had passed, and I did not know what day it was. The phone rang all day and all night, but I could not force myself to answer it.

I just needed some peace and quiet, and I wanted to die. Never in a million years did I think that this would happen to me. I could not eat, sleep, or bathe. All I did was watch that disgusting sex movie over and over again and cry. I felt like killing myself, but what would happen to my baby girl? Who would she have then? A dead mother, one who committed suicide, and a fucking faggot for a father.

Thank God for the Greens, because right now I needed a guardian angel, and Mama Green was just that. I could not care for my daughter right now, and Mama Green knew that. She left me a message telling me to take all the time that I needed, and that's just what I did.

Chapter Eleven

Sorrow

Weeks had passed and still I had no contact with anyone. I had lost a lot of weight, and my hair was a hot mess. I don't know the last time I had taken a bath or eaten for that matter. And just when I thought shit could not get any worse, Mink was standing over me, calling out my fucking name. I closed my eyes, because I just knew that I was fucking dreaming. But when I opened them again that faggot was still standing there, so I got up and just started swinging.

I could not believe that this bastard had the nerve to come back to this house, our house where he fucked Tyrell, in our bed no less. I was screaming and crying, calling Mink all types of faggots, sissies, and punk bitches. The whole time that I was carrying on, he just stood there taking everything that I had to give him. That did not make me feel any better, though. It only made me feel much worse. You never believe that this shit could happen to you, but it did happen to me, and I wanted someone else to feel my pain. All Mink kept saying was, "Jazmine, I am so sorry, baby, please forgive me. Then he said, "I never meant to hurt you or for you to find out this way that I sleep with men. Please just listen to what I have to say, and then I promise you that I will leave. Jazmine, I am not going to make excuses for anything that I have done, because first and foremost I am a man."

I screamed, "A man who fucks other men! Nigger, please, if you're a fucking man then I'm a fucking man."

He yelled out, "Goddammit, Jazmine, just let me finish, and then I will be gone." When I looked over at him, there were tears flowing down Mink's face. So I just sat back and waited to hear what he had to say to me, my gay baby daddy. How could my fiancé, my soul mate, the love of my fucking life, how could he be a butt bandit?

So I said, "You know what, Mink, okay, just get this shit over with, and tell me what made you a flaming faggot."

He looked over at me with hate in his eyes but I did not care, the feeling was mutual. I hated him right then too. He started off with, "I have been having sex with men since I was seven years old. My parent's friend first introduced me to the feelings that I have had all these years. I have tried to suppress my urges, but goddammit I just can't."

I yelled out, "Yes you can, you fucking faggot. Mink, you could have fought the desires if you wanted to. What about Diamond, and what about me? You did not give a fuck about us, even after I told you that bastard raped Nina. You still bent over, and let that motherfucker put his dick up in you. Mink, you can finish your story, but I hate you, and nothing you say or do will ever change that. Now please go ahead, and tell your story but make it quick, nigger." I had a half of a blunt in my ashtray, so I lit it up, and just sat back to listen to the rest of this fucked-up gay tragedy.

Mink said, "Reverend Brooks is my parent's friend who took away my childhood."

I was sorry, but I had to interrupt him once again. "Reverend Brooks, the preacher who was going to perform our wedding ceremony? Oh my fucking God, this shit is sicker than I thought."

Mink just kept right on talking, like he did not even hear me speaking. "Reverend Brooks was always very nice to me when I was a kid. He was always giving me nice gifts and bags of candy. He was always there when I needed someone to talk to, and a shoulder to cry on. I guess I was a very needy child, and I required a lot of attention. He just always seemed to know what I needed, at the right time.

"One day in his office he told me to come and have a seat on his lap. When I sat down I felt that his dick was hard and it scared me. At that time I really did not understand sex at all, but I knew this was wrong. Then he put his hand on my penis, and started to rub it round and round. I did not know that he had my pants down, or that his were down either until he pushed me on my knees and put his dick in my mouth. He started moving my head back and forth, and he was making all these weird sounds and calling me his special little boy.

"After he came in my mouth, he told me to bend over his table, and that he would make me feel good the way that I made him feel good. Then he put his dick in my asshole real fast. Jazz, it hurt so bad, so I started screaming out in pain and begging him to stop. He put his hand over my mouth, and fucked me until he came all over again. When he was done,

I was crying and shaking all over. I did not know what to do, and all I wanted was my mother. Reverend Brook's wiped off his dick and then he went into the bathroom, and when he came out he had a wet rag to clean me up with.

"When he touched me it hurt real bad, and my butt was burning, and when he pulled the rag away I saw blood on it. When I saw the blood I thought I was dying, and that scared me even more, so I started crying even harder. He told me that this was nothing for me to be afraid of, that it would stop bleeding in a little while. Then he said that God did not mind if we did special things in private together. But we had to keep it a secret because if we told anyone what we did, that God would be mad at us. Then he asked me, if I wanted God to be mad at me? I told him no, then he kissed me on my lips real gentle, and told me not to worry. He said that everything was going to be all right in due time, because he would take care of everything.

"When my mother picked me up later that afternoon, I was very quiet on the ride back home. She asked me what was wrong, and I told her that I was just tired. Who knows, she probably had other things on her mind that day, because she did not press the issue. I was praying that she would ask me again, but she didn't. And as the years wore on, I don't know, Jazz, I guess that I started to like it, and I just become accustomed to it. "Then when I reached puberty all my friends were fucking all the hot little bitches from around our way. So I went along with them, and did what they were doing. Junior high school and high school were hard for me, but I hid my secret very well. No one ever found out, that is until now, so I was free to continue to have sex with Reverend Brook's in secret. Shit, to me what we were doing was normal, and I never told a soul about it until now.

"When I graduated from high school I worked at the church for the summer. I worked with the children in the summer camp so practically every day Reverend Brooks and I got to play our special game. One day I opened up the reverend's door and little Tommy was in there, bent over in my usual spot."

Now up until this point I was quiet while Mink told this fucked-up horror story, but I screamed out, "Tommy the reverend's son? Oh my God, Mink, he was fucking his own son?"

Mink looked over at me and said, "Yes, Jazz, he was fucking his own son."

"Mink, so you're telling me that pervert was having sex with his own damn son?" Mink looked over at me and said, "Yes, Jazmine, his own damn son, now please let me finish my story."

So I sat back, closed my eyes, and waited to hear how the rest of this fucked-up drama played out.

Mink lowered his head, and said, "You had to see the expression on their faces, Jazz. It was almost scary, like a deer caught in someone's headlights."

I said, "Mink, I did see that expression, remember?"

He ignored me and just kept right on talking. "I still have nightmares about that shit all the time. Anyway after that incident, I finally realized what we had been doing for all these years was wrong. So I told him that we had to stop having sex with each other. And I told him that if I ever thought that he was still fucking his son, or fucking any other child in the church, I would go straight to the police. He looked me in my eyes and knew that I was dead serious, and then he told me that he would stop and never do it again for as long as he lived.

"For four more years I watched him to make sure that he kept his word, until I just stopped going to church all together."

I asked Mink, "Well, why did you say that you wanted him to perform our wedding, if he did all that sick and disgusting shit to you?"

"Jazmine, I did not want him anywhere near you or me for that matter. It was my parent's idea. Jazmine, what was I supposed to say when they suggested that he perform the services? Um excuse me Ma, Dad, your friend started fucking me when I was seven years old, so I don't think he should perform my wedding ceremony? I couldn't say that, so instead I said nothing. After I saw the reverend with his son that day I tried to steer clear of men forever, and then I met Tyrell one night at a party. And right after me and Tyrell started fucking around is when I met and fell in love with you. I loved having sex with Tyrell, but my feelings for you were growing each and every day.

"I had never met anyone like you before in my life, and it just felt right between us. Once we moved in together I tried to break it off with Tyrell for good, but I was caught between a rock and a hard place. Tyrell would not take no for an answer, and then you told me that shit that went down between Tyrell and Nina. Jazz, it was too late by the time that I spoke to you that night, because as soon as me and Tyrell got to Virginia we had sex, so you see the dirty deed was already done.

"I never meant to hurt you, Jazmine, or have sex with Tyrell ever again. We were both drunk the night that I told him Nina had HIV, and it just happened. We had already gotten busy earlier when we first touched down, so what was one more time? Jazz, who knows why I fucked him again, maybe I felt that I deserved to die because of how I was treating you all this time?"

This shit was too much for one person to handle, and I was too upset to even speak. So I did the only thing that I could do, I pressed play on the motherfucking DVD player and I sat back and waited. When I heard Mink suck in his breath I turned around, and just looked at the expression on his face. The funny thing was he really looked surprised, like he did not know where this movie had came from, or that he was on it.

Then he yelled out, "That son of a bitch!" At that moment I knew that Tyrell had put this shit in our house so that I could find it one day.

I could not believe this shit, so I asked Mink, "Tyrell put this movie here didn't he?"

He did not even have to answer me because in my heart I already knew the truth. This was one twisted nightmare that I really wanted to wake up from immediately. I saw the vein in Mink's forehead throbbing, and at that moment I knew that there was going to be trouble.

Mink kept saying, "I don't believe that he did this shit. I told him that I could not deal with him like that anymore and he goes and does this. I'm going to kill his ass."

I was just staring at him, and Mink looked like he was ready to explode. He looked at me and told me that he had something to take care of. And then he told me that he would call me later, and then he walked out the door and out of my life. All night long I sat up and wondered where Mink was at, and what he was doing. I also thought about my baby girl Diamond. I had not called my daughter in over three weeks, and I felt like a bad mother.

So the next morning I called Mama Green and I apologized to her for staying away so long. She told me that she knew I was going through some rough times right now, but God would see me through it. I told her sometime within the next week I was going to stop by and get my child. She told me not to worry about a thing, and then she put Diamond on the phone. When I heard her voice on the line I told my baby that I loved her, and that I was going to see her real soon.

Diamond made some gurgling sounds, and then I heard her say "ma ma" as clear as day. My baby had said her first words, and I wasn't there with her. Shit, now I really felt like a bad mother, and the next thing you know Mama Green was back on the line. I asked her, "Did Diamond just say ma ma?"

She said, "Yes, baby, you heard right. She has been saying ma ma for two days now, but I did not call you because I knew that you were dealing with something major in your life right now."

Ma Green told me that she loved me and for me to stay strong, and she said that if I needed a friend, God was always there to listen.

When we hung up I got down on my knees and prayed for forgiveness and the strength to move on with my life. When I was done my heart felt light and I just exhaled. Then I decided to wash my hair and body because I was a funky monkey, and it was making me sick to my stomach. When I was done I said to myself, "Damn it feels good to be clean." I cleaned my house from top to bottom and front to back. My shit was a hot mess and it was a damn shame, and then when I was done with all of that I made a can of chicken noodle soup and a bologna sandwich to eat.

I looked in the mirror on my wall, and I did not like what I saw. I looked like a walking skeleton. My face, hair, nails, and toes were a hot mess. I needed some help. I had lost massive weight, and my eyes and cheeks were sucked in like I was smoking crack. I was tore up from the floor up, but today I was going to do something about it. The first step was going to get my daughter, from her grandparent's house. After I got my hair, nails, and toes done, I felt a little bit like a human being again, and then I went and picked up Diamond. That day I took my life back and I started doing yoga every morning and every evening to cleanse my mind, body, and soul. It could have been a mind thing, but I believed that yoga was helping me, and at least I was calm.

Right before my eyes a month had passed, and I was finally starting to get my life back on track. I went to see my sister and nephew for a week, and the time we spent together was great. Little Ty loved Diamond so much, and he kept calling her his little princess. We really had a good time over there. All we did was eat, sleep, and watch television. It was a peaceful time, and I was starting to feel some type of joy. When we went back home, I checked the answering machine to see if Mink had left me a message, but there wasn't one.

I was starting to get worried, but I did not want to call anyone just yet and worry him or her. I had not heard from Mink since I showed him the gay sex DVD, and that was over a month ago. Shit, I did not know why I even cared, but I did care, and I was so mad at myself. Love makes you do some crazy things, and I was still crazy in love with Mink. After all the shit that he did to me, my stupid ass was still in love with him.

All I had was Diamond, and she was growing so fast, and she had just said her second set of words. She said da da, now ain't that some shit? I was with her every day, but she still called out for her daddy. Yes, she said ma ma first, but so what, I did not want to hear her call out to her daddy, ever. I knew that in the next few weeks my baby girl would be walking on her own instead of holding onto things, and then her first birthday would be approaching.

Time was flying, but I still could not get over Mink fucking with men. I don't know what was worse—walking in on Mink and Tyrell, or Mink telling me that fucked-up story about the reverend, or me seeing that sick gay sex movie. My life was so messed up, and throughout everything that had happened I still had not heard from Nina. God only knows where my girl was at, or what she was doing. I just hoped that she was alive, and doing as well as could be expected.

Mink was officially declared a missing person. The Greens had filed a missing person's report two days earlier. Everyone was worried, because we all knew that Mink would not have missed Diamond's first birthday. We gave her a small party at the Green's house, just family because nobody was in the mood for a big affair. I prayed for Mink and Nina every night, wishing and hoping that they just return home. I just wanted these two people who I loved and missed the most in my life to come back to me one day. I was so tired of all this sorrow; I just wanted to live my life in peace.

I had a couple of dollars saved over from my stashing days, so I was not lacking money. But the house was driving me fucking crazy, and I knew that I needed to get a job. I enrolled Diamond in a day care center not too far from my house, and then I went job hunting. All I had was my GED, so I didn't have much to choose from, and my skills were very limited. But if someone gave me a chance, then I would not let him or her down. Several days had passed when the devil started moving in on me. He was trying to break my sprit. The devil was telling me that no one was going to hire me, and I had started to believe my negative thoughts.

I had just about given up all hope on finding a job when I was called back for a receptionist position at a doctor's office, and I got the job. I would be working five days a week, and no weekends. The pay was not the best, but it would give me something to do instead of sitting at home depressed, all day every day. My boss was a very nice African woman named Doctor Okonkwo. She was a single parent of two boys, and she just seemed to enjoy life. Her personality was beautiful, and she just made me feel good to be alive. I guess God knew that I needed a boost in my life, and I welcomed her joy with open arms.

Every day when she came to work she would bring coffee and a quotation. Sometimes I did not know what they meant, but other times her quotes were just what I needed to hear at the time. Diamond was progressing well in day care, her speech was excellent, and all she talked about was her daddy. She had Mink's picture on her dresser, and every time she asked me about him, I did not know what to tell her. Detectives Munch and Terry were assigned to Mink's case. They came by almost every week ever since his parents had filed the missing persons report, but they never had any new information about his disappearance.

A few months before Thanksgiving, India called to see how Diamond and I were doing. I was very happy to hear from my girl, because I had not spoken to her in quite awhile. We talked for a little while, and then she told me that Benny was still in rehab but he was coming along fine. I told her that was good news, and then I told her about Nina's disappearing act. India said that she was very sorry to hear that then she screamed out, "Oh my God, Jazz, turn on your television, turn to channel five news."

When I turned to channel five, I could not believe my fucking eyes. There was a picture of Mink, and the news reporter said that he was holding Reverend Brooks hostage inside his church.

The reporter was saying, "If you are just tuning in, Jonathon Mink Green, our suspect in last week's slaying of Tyrell Henderson, has now taken a hostage. He is holding the Reverend Gary Brooks of the Queens Baptist Church prisoner. Hostage negotiator David Johnson of the Queens task force has just arrived on the scene. Stay tuned, and we will give you more of this shocking story when we return."

I could not believe this shit. Mink had killed Tyrell last week, and now he was going to kill that sick perverted bastard for what he did to him all those years ago. The whole time that I was watching he news, India was yelling out my name. When I finally come back to earth, and realized that I was still on the phone with Indy. I told her that I would call her back and hung up. When the line was clear, the first person I called was Shonda. I told her to turn her television on and for her to watch Fox Five News, and then I told her that I would call her back later. She asked me what was wrong, and I screamed out, "Bitch, just watch the damn news!"

Next I called the Greens and told them the tragic news. After we watched the news together for a while we were all at a loss for words, so I told them that I would call them back later on. I knew just how they felt, because I felt the exact same way, and the news anchor did not have much more to report. She only said that Mink had shot Tyrell four times in the head at point-blank range last Tuesday. The police knew that Mink had committed the murder, because there had been a struggle in the house, and Mink's fingerprints were all over the apartment.

How in the hell didn't anyone know about this shit? The news anchor answered the question for me before I could even finish my train of thought. There were so many fingerprints in Tyrell's apartment that it was basically a process of elimination, and at the end of the list there was Mink. Mink was the last known person to see Tyrell alive, and in their last moments together Mink killed Tyrell in a fit of uncontrollable rage. Tyrell's next-door neighbors had seen Mink and Tyrell go inside his apartment together, and they did not notice anything out of the ordinary. Then they heard a lot of noise and banging like a fight was going on, then they heard four gunshots, and then silence.

Now from what I could gather, Mink was in a hysterical state of mind and he was not listening to anyone. Negotiator Johnson was inside the room trying to calm him down, but so far nothing was working. At that moment my telephone rang, and when I answered it a Detective Jamison was on the line. He asked me if I was aware of the situation with Mink, and I told him I was. Then I asked him if there was something I could do. He said that my child's father wanted to talk to me, and then he asked me if that was okay with me. He said that if it was okay, he would patch me through to Mink.

I said okay, and then I heard no more from the detective. I heard three clicks, and then I heard Mink's voice on the line. I cleared my throat, and then I said, "Hello, Mink."

"Jazz, is that really you?"

"Yes baby, it's me. Mink, you have to let that bastard go. I know he hurt you but this will not make it right."

"Jazmine, I killed Tyrell for what he did to you, Jazz I killed him for what he did to us."

"I know, baby, but you have to let the reverend go."

"Jazmine, you were never supposed to see that movie. I didn't even know that Tyrell was taping us until after he had already did it."

"Baby, it's okay, but you still have to let that man go, and then you can go and get some help. "

"Help, what kind of help can they give a faggot like me? It's all his fault, and this pervert has got to die because he made me this way. Jazmine, it's all his fault, and he is going to pay for it with his life. "

"Mink, you have to listen to me. Yes, what he did was wrong, very wrong, but you have to let him go." I was trying to calm him down, but it was not working. Mink, was incoherent and I feared for the worst.

"Fuck that shit. Jazmine, this bastard had the nerve to look me in my face and say that he did nothing wrong. I told him that I would let him go if he confessed about what he did to me as a child, and he said that he had nothing to confess. So we are not leaving this room until he tells me the fucking truth or so help me God I will put a bullet in his head. Jazmine, he has ten minutes to open his damn mouth, and if he does not tell the truth about what he did to me and those other little boys, I swear, I will blow his fucking head off."

"Mink, the police will kill you if you don't let him go."

"So what? I am dead to you already. Jazmine, what do I really have to live for?"

"Diamond, you have her to live for. And what about your parents, and the rest of your family?"

"Jazmine, none of that matters to me without you. I love my baby girl but she is better off without me, and my parents do not want a faggot for a son."

I was crying, trying to get him to listen to me, but he was not hearing me at all. I said, "Mink, I still love you, so please don't do this. We can try to work everything out, but you have to let him go first."

Mink laughed and said, "Jazmine, that was sweet of you, but I am a homo, and you do not really want me in your life. So they might as well kill me now."

Next thing I knew, I was talking to someone else. The person identified himself as negotiator Johnson. He asked me if I thought that Mink was serious.

I told him yes, he was very serious. I told him the reverend had molested Mink for a number of years as a child, and now Mink wanted his revenge. Negotiator Johnson then told me that they were going to have to take Mink down soon if he did not surrender.

"Please don't kill Mink," I said. "He has been under a lot of stress lately, and all he really needs is some help." I heard Mink in the background, screaming that he had to talk to me again.

When he came on the line he was crying, and then he said, "Jazz, I love you," over and over again. I told him that I loved him too, and then I heard a dial tone. I sat holding the receiver in my hand, crying, and just continued to watch the news. Then I heard the sound of gunshots.

The anchorwoman said they would take a break, and when she came back she would give us the shocking conclusion to this unbelievable story. Five minutes felt like an eternity, and I was dying inside. When she came back on the air she told the world that the Reverend Gary Brooks was dead, and his killer, Jonathon Mink Green, was wounded in the upper chest. She said that Mink was being rushed to Queens General, and his chance for survival did not look good. I dressed Diamond and myself then we flew out of the door.

When I reached the hospital, Detective Munch and Terry were already there, as well as the whole Green clan. I just fell into Pop Green's arms and cried. Miracle came over and took Diamond to the other waiting area to get away from the nightmare that was taking place right before our eyes. Once they were out of hearing range the detectives asked me if I knew why Mink would kill his friend Tyrell and his former minister. I looked over at

Mink's parents, and then I told the Greens to have a seat. Once they were seated, I told them Mink's unbelievable tale.

When I was finished my story, everyone was staring at me in a state of shock. No one could believe the words that I had just spoken, and at that moment Mink's doctor came out to talk to us. He said that they had removed the two bullets from his chest, and that the surgery had gone well. He felt that Mink would live, but he would need a lot of rest during his recovery because he had lost a lot of blood. We were all very happy that Mink would heal from the gunshot wounds, but we were also sad. The detectives were charging Mink with premeditated murder for killing Tyrell and that pervert Reverend Brooks.

Chapter Twelve

The Trial

It took Mink a few weeks to recover, and when he was well enough to be released from the hospital he was taken straight to Rikers Island. His family and I found him the best criminal lawyer that money could buy, and we were all just praying for a miracle. Shane Morgan was a new hotshot lawyer from the streets of Harlem where he fought his way out of poverty, and now he was a successful defense attorney.

Mr. Morgan felt confident about Mink's case from the very beginning, and he said that he would have Mink plead temporary insanity. If all went well at the trial, Mink probably would not have to do any jail time, but some time in a state hospital might be good for him. Many different doctors were called in to figure out Mink's state of mind at the time of the shooting. And they all agreed that when Mink killed those men his frame of mind was not stable; they said that Mink was in distress.

Weeks had gone by, and no one knew what the outcome would be of the murder trial, but Mink's lawyer was leaning toward a not guilty verdict. He said that if he was found guilty, Mink was only going to have to spend about six months to a year in a state mental institution. Maybe he would only serve a few months inside, just to get the help that he needed. We were all hoping and praying for the best. Thank God I was finished with my case for shooting Mink, because I could not handle all of this shit at once. I plead guilty, was given community service and had to pay a fine.

Mink would not press charges against me for shooting him, so I only received three years probation for having the gun. And that was a slap on the wrist. It could have been much worse for me so I was truly grateful. The prosecutor started off his case against Mink by introducing a lot of bullshit evidence, all about what led up to the mayhem that took place that night.

They called me to testify against Mink, but I told them nothing. I looked right at the jury and denied everything, and I did not care if they knew that I was lying. I would do anything to keep Mink out of jail, because that is not where he needed to be.

Reverend Brooks' wife testified that her husband was a good, holy, and Christian man. She said that he did not deserve to die the way that he did, and then she talked about all the work that he did to help out the community children. She talked about all the help that he gave the children of his congregation on a regular basis, and then his son Tommy took the stand. Surprisingly, Tommy told all about the abuse that his father inflicted on him over a long period of time. He still did not understand why his father felt the need to hurt him the way that he did, and why his father never wanted to stop. Tommy was so emotional that eventually he broke down on the witness stand and just cried like a baby.

After his damaging testimony, the prosecution had no more witnesses to produce. Everyone in the courtroom was stunned after what Tommy had just revealed—everyone except us. People all around us were whispering in their seats, "Not the man of the cloth! Not the man that everyone loved and trusted with their children, not Reverend Brooks!" No one wanted to believe it, but everyone knew that it had to be true. The defense started off by calling several other young men from the church who came forward with their testimony of the sexual abuse that Reverend Brooks had inflicted on them.

A lot of these men were unstable, and their lives were in shambles. Many of them could not function on a day-to-day basis in this cruel and unjust world. But the really twisted shit came out when little Bobby Turner, a nine-year-old boy from the church, took the stand. He said that his abuse started a month ago, and Mrs. Gloria Brooks was the one who took him to the reverend. Bobby said that she would sit there and watch while the reverend raped him over and over again. After his testimony the Greens testified, and anyone else who knew Mink as a person, not the monster that the prosecution tried to make him out to be.

One minute Mink's case looked very bad, and then the next minute everything looked like it would work out fine. In the end all we could do was pray that Mink was given another chance, and that he would get the help that he needed. After all of the testimony, the defense had called their last witness in the case of the murder of Reverend Brooks. Next the prosecution brought in all the evidence about Tyrell's case. Mink's lawyer said for us not to worry, he said that he would introduce Tyrell's medical condition and his knowledge of it.

Tyrell did have the HIV virus, and being that he knew this before he slept with Mink that last time at our home Mink was also a victim, and that worked well in his favor. Tyrell did not have any family, so there was nobody to come forth in his defense. His parents were both killed a car accident in 1997, and he was their only child. After their death he lived a sad and lonely life. We did not know if that was good or bad for Mink, but we would find out soon enough. A little while later in the trial we got the shock of our lives, when Mr. Morgan said that he had a surprise witness. On the third week of trial Mr. Morgan called Nina Gonzalez to the stand.

Unknown to any of us, Mr. Morgan had tracked Nina down and enrolled her in a drug treatment program in Queens. The reason why he did not mention it to us was because Nina asked him not to tell anyone that he had found her. She told him that would be the only way that she would take the stand and tell her story, so he agreed to her terms. When Nina walked in I got so emotional that I had to leave the courtroom. When I returned from the bathroom, Nina was already done with her testimony.

She was waiting for me in the hallway, and as I walked toward her all she said was, "Jazmine, I am so sorry."

I told her that it was all right, and for her not to worry about anything. I told her just to get herself together, and to come home safe to her family. I don't know how long we stayed in the hallway, but when I finally looked up everyone else was coming out of the courtroom. Mink came over to us and gave Nina a hug and a kiss, and told her thank you. And then with tears in his eyes, he walked away from us with his head down. I told the Greens that I would call them later on, and then Nina and I grabbed a bite to eat not too far from the courthouse at a place called The Square. After we finished eating, Nina said that she had to get back to the program, so we did not get to talk about a lot of things, but what was there to say?

I dropped Nina off at her destination and went home to get some much-needed rest. I picked Diamond up from the day care center, and then we went home for me to get ready for another day of courtroom bullshit. When I got to the courthouse the next day, closing arguments had already begun. It was a very long day, and then two days after the jury deliberation the verdict was finally in. The judge said, "Jonathon Mink Green, will you please rise?" I did not realize that I was holding my breath until I heard the words, "Not guilty on all counts."

All I remember is Mama Green yelling out, "Thank you God, my baby is free." It was a happy day for everyone, so we all went out to celebrate. After we ate I left to go and pick up Diamond from the day care center, and then I went home to relax. That same night Mink called me and asked if he could come over and spend some time with Diamond. I told him sure. that it was no problem. When Mink arrived, Diamond was so happy to see her daddy that she ran straight into his arms. She gave him lots of hugs and kisses, and when I looked over at Mink he had tears in his eyes.

He carried Diamond to her room, and that's where they stayed until she fell asleep that night. After he tucked her in, he came into the living room and asked me if we could talk. I told him of course, but when he opened his mouth no words came out, so he started all over again.

"Jazmine, I know in my heart that there is no chance in hell that you would ever take me back, I know that. Especially after finding out the things that you know about me, so I am not going to play myself and ask, but I want to be in Diamond's life.

"I do not want to go to court for visitation rights, so please don't make me. Please just think about what I am asking you, I would really appreciate that from the bottom of my heart You don't have to answer me right now, just know that no matter what decision you make. I will always love you, and I will always cherish our memories with all my heart and soul. I am sorry about all the pain that I have caused you, believe me, I never meant to hurt you."

For the life of me I did not understand why Mink thought that I would not let him see our child. He knew I was not like that, even after all the drama that he put me through. I would never hold our child over his head. It would not be fair to Diamond or Mink, and I loved her too much to hurt her that way. A few minutes went by, and then I told Mink not too worry about seeing our daughter. I told him she would always be in his life.

After I said my piece to him, Mink looked real sad, and then he said, "Jazmine, I have the monster." I looked at him wide-eyed, and he said, "Yes, Jazz, I have full-blown AIDS." As I sat there listening to him talk all I could do was cry, and then Mink said, "Jazz, I am dying," and then he cried too. I felt so bad for him, but what could I do? Just about everyone that I loved was dead or either dying from the same damn disease. Soon all I would have is my precious daughter, and my sister, Shonda, and her family. All I could do was hold Mink until he calmed down, which seemed to take all night.

The next morning was Saturday, and when we got up I cooked breakfast for my family. Mink and Diamond played in the living room all morning, and then they watched cartoons together. When we were done eating I got Diamond dressed to take her to the park so she could play with the other children, and get some fresh air. Mink said that he had to go and attend his support group for people living with AIDS. The support group seemed to be helping him sort out his problems, and I hoped that everything worked out for him.

I prayed to God every night for him to take the love that I have for Mink out of my heart, but the feelings wouldn't go away. My love for him was strong, and for him I was weak—but not weak enough to risk my life. When we got home from the park, I made dinner for me and Diamond, and then we watched *Toy Story 2* until we both fell asleep. The next weekend Mink came and picked up Diamond and took her to his parent's house for his weekend visit. Mink had moved back into his parent's house after all the bullshit in his life, and the Greens were trying to cope with the fact that their longtime friend had violated their son so many years ago.

Times were hard for everyone, and it seemed like Pop Green was taking this situation the hardest. Pop Green and Reverend Brooks had grown up together, and now he knew that one of his oldest and dearest friends had almost ruined his son's life. Mink's parents had even started attending the support group with him some nights; they were trying to put their life back together after the trial. Sometimes I thought that I should attend the meetings too, but I really did not want to get involved in that part of Mink's new life—a young black man living with full-blown AIDS.

One morning Mama Green called and said that she was going to stop by for a visit. It was going on lunchtime, so I made a grilled chicken salad and some ice-cold lemonade. When she arrived her grandbaby was so happy to see her, and Mama Green was just as happy to see Diamond. We talked for a while, playing catch-up in each other's lives, then I suggested that we sit down to eat. The chicken salad was good, and we both ate a lot while Diamond ate a peanut butter and jelly sandwich with a cup of strawberry milk.

When we finished eating I went to put Diamond down for a nap, and then Mama Green and I watched *Claudine*. I loved this movie; Nina and I watched it all the time growing up. It was always one of the Sunday afternoon movies on channel five. James Earl Jones and Diahann Carroll gave wonderful performances, and by the end of the movie we were both crying.

Mama Green looked over at me and said, "Baby I know right now you don't know which way is up. But Jazmine, my God sits high, but he sees low. So you just keep trusting in the Lord and raising that beautiful little girl just the way you're doing. You will see that in the end, everything will work out just fine."

By now, the tears were flowing down my face. So I excused myself and went to wipe my eyes and get a glass of water. When I returned to the living room, Mama Green was standing up looking out of the living room window. She must have felt my presence, because she never turned around, but her words just started flowing.

"Jazmine, Mink is not taking all of this well." Then she turned and looked at me. "He has given up on life. The only time that he leaves the house is when he comes over here to get Diamond, or when he goes to a meeting. The only reason I knew that he was still going to the meetings at all is because his father and I started going with him. Truthfully, I do not think that the meetings are helping any of us, but we are doing it together and that's what matters the most.

"Mink does not say anything to us at all, and all that does is make Mack angry, and all I do is pray. I pray but nothing seems to help, and now I am testing my own faith. I know God loves us, but I don't understand how he could let this happen to us. Jazmine, I am sorry to be telling you all of this, then I turn around and tell you to trust in the Lord but I don't know what to think anymore."

I told her that she did not have to explain anything to me, and that I understood what she was going through because I was feeling the exact same way. She looked at me, and said, "Mink cannot see life without you in it. Jazmine, we told him that he had to go on with his life, but he said not without you in it. He won't take his medication anymore, he is not eating or sleeping, and the only time he bathes is when he comes over here to see you. Jazmine, we don't know what to do anymore.

"Baby, I am so scared for him, can you please just talk to him for me? He always seemed to listen to you, and if you talk to him now maybe you can find out what he is thinking."

I did not want to talk to Mink at all but what could I say? I said, "Mama, I will call his cell phone tonight."

She looked at me, and said, "Jazmine, his cell phone has been cut off since before the trial." Nothing else shocked me, but Mink had that same telephone number for the past five years. He said that he was going to have that same number until the day that he died, so I guess that he was almost right. Mama Green left about an hour after that. She said that she had a nice time with us, and that she would call me real soon.

I felt so alone after Mink's mother left. Nobody but Nina would understand me. I had only spoken to my sister girl three times since the trial, but she sounded like she was doing okay. She said that she was going to take it slow, but she was very optimistic about her recovery. She wanted to get clean for the right reasons now, herself. Before she had wanted to do it for me and my family, but now Nina Simone Gonzalez wanted to get clean for herself. I was so proud of her. I told her to stay strong and to keep the faith.

Right about then I needed Nina's strength, so I said a prayer for
guidance, and then I waited another hour before calling Mink's house.
Miracle answered the phone on the second ring, and after we talked for a
minute or two she called Mink to the phone. I heard him come on the line
and say hello. I was nervous as hell, but I had to do what I had to do. So I
said, "Hello, Mink, how are you?"

"Jazmine, is everything all right with Diamond?"

"Yes, Mink, everything is fine with Diamond, I was just calling to see
how you were doing. We don't really talk anymore, so I decided to give you
a call."

"I didn't know that you had anything to say to me, if it wasn't about
Diamond."

"Mink, that's not true. Regardless of what's happened between us, we
will always be a part of each other's lives. And yes I will always love you, so
stop talking crazy and tell me what's really going on."

"Not much, Jazz, I'm just chilling, trying to maintain, you know."

"That's good to hear, but what are you doing for money? I know you
are not still out there hustling."

"No, I left that shit alone quite a while ago. You know that I had a
mean stash put away, and with me having this disease I can receive SSI so
I looked into that, and I was also thinking about enrolling in college."

"Mink, that's wonderful, what will you major in?"

"I don't know, maybe I'll take a business class, or a writing course. Jazz,
you know writing short stories, and poetry is my shit."

"Yes I know, Mink. You did write some nice poems when we were
together. Mink, you know you have to keep your head up, and keep thinking
positive, right? That way you can do anything that you want to do in your
life."

Mink said, "Shit, this is not a life, taking sixty fucking pills a day."
Out of nowhere Mink got very angry and said, "Jazz, I am real tired right
now so I will talk to you later. I will call Diamond tomorrow, so give her
a kiss for me." With no goodbye he just hung up on me. Something did
not feel right, and I had a sharp pain in the pit of my stomach. But with
everything that was going on, queasiness was the least of my worries. I
took two aspirin and called it a night, wondering what tomorrow would
bring my way.

Chapter Thirteen

Surprises

The holidays rolled around, and we all had a lot to be thankful for. So for Thanksgiving everyone gathered at the Green's house for a real holiday meal. Shonda, Michael, and little Ty came over to celebrate with us, and we had a great time together. Nina was given a holiday pass, so she was there with us as well, and it felt great to have her home again. The food was great, and it felt so good to be around family and friends. Nina looked real good, too. She looked very healthy, and she had put on a little bit of weight.

I was glad that she was finally taking care of herself, and that she left the drugs alone for good. On another positive note, Mink had started college, and he seemed to be very happy, and as for me I was still working for Doctor Okonkwo. She was still crazy as ever, but I loved her for giving me all that time off during Mink's trial. Even though I had just started working for her, she did not even think twice. She told me to take all the time that I needed, and when I was ready to come back to work that my job would be there waiting for me.

After dinner Shonda and Michael announced that they had a surprise for us. They told us that they were getting married on New Year's Eve. Everyone was overjoyed, but the only one who was not smiling was Mink. He seemed to have a dark and scary look in his eyes, and he just looked spaced out. Pop Green asked them what was the rush, and Michael said there was no rush. He said that he loved Shonda and little Ty very much, so there was no reason to put the wedding on hold and wait. I was so happy for them, and my wheels were already turning. I was going to give them a nice wedding reception, and Mama Green and Nina would help me put it together.

Nina had to be back to the program by nine, and little Ty and Diamond were both tired, so a little while later we all left. Mama Green made sure that we had bags of food for days, and then Shonda dropped Nina off at the program and Diamond and me off at my house. After I gave Diamond her bath she was asleep in seconds. But I could not sleep, so I stayed up for awhile thinking and making plans for the reception. I would have to talk to Michael, because I needed to know who they wanted to invite from their jobs.

The next day I called Michael and told him my great idea. He was very happy, and he said that he would write the list and drop it off on his way home from work. With all that taken care of, now all I had to do was find a reception hall. And then it hit me like a ton of bricks. The wedding reception would be held at Mars 2112, the same place that my reception would have been if I had not found out that Mink slept with men. A few hours later I was talking to Mama Green on the telephone, and I asked her if she knew of a good catering service.

Mama said, "Child, please, you don't have to spend good money on no catering service. I will do the cooking myself, and Miracle will help me. Just give me your menu, and let me know how many people will be invited, and we will do the rest."

I said, "Okay, Mama," and I told her thank you.

She said, "Child, please, we are family; you don't have to thank me for nothing."

I told her that I would drop the list off to her before the week was out, and I could not wait for the wedding to take place. We talked for a little while longer, and then we hung up. That same night Michael brought his list over to me. He had seventy-five people on it and I had about the same amount of people on my list. So there would be one hundred and fifty people who would be coming to an extravagant wedding reception.

The menu would consist of all kinds of chicken. There would be fried chicken, baked chicken, smothered chicken, and curry chicken. There would be collared greens, cabbage, string beans, and macaroni and cheese. Mama was making candied yams, ribs, biscuits, and ham, and all kinds of dessert. Nina and I would be Shonda and Michael's witnesses at city hall. Shonda's wedding dress was a beige satin number with a semi-long train, and she was going to look stunning in it. Then after the wedding the dress would detach into a mini evening gown so she could get her party on.

Michael would be wearing a black tuxedo with a beige cummerbund, and Nina and I would be wearing peach, Shonda's favorite color. Ever since we were kids, Shonda had always loved that color. Shonda had no idea about the reception; she just thought that we would have a small dinner at a restaurant downtown. I could not wait to see the expression on her face. I knew that she was going to be very surprised.

Christmas came, and Diamond opened her many Christmas presents. Then we headed over to the Green's house for Mama's special Christmas dinner.

When we got there I noticed right away that Mink was very distant and withdrawn, but I left it alone for the moment. I told myself that I would investigate the matter later on—right now I was there to have a good time. After we all got our stomachs full, I asked Mink to step outside with me on the porch so we could talk. Once we were outside I lit up my blunt and Mink if he wanted some, he told me no. "Jazz, I'm good. You know drugs was never my thing."

"Mink, what is your thing then, and why are you so damn quiet today? What's the matter with you?"

"Life, that's what's the matter with me. Jazmine, I just can't cope with this shit anymore." I guess he looked away from me because he did not want me to see the tears in his eyes, but I had already saw them forming.

"Mink, I know this is hard for you, But you can't let it beat you, don't let it get the best of you."

He looked at me and said, "Jazmine, it is beating me, and there is nothing that I can do about it. I have tried to fight it, but I can't and now I am ready to give up."

"Mink, look at me, where does that leave Diamond?" He could not even answer me; he just turned and looked away. "Mink, do you hear me talking to you, I said what about our daughter?"

"Jazmine, I just don't know what to do anymore. I feel like the meetings are not working, and I hate looking at myself in the mirror every day." He looked me in my face and asked me, "Jazmine, what am I supposed to do?"

For once, I was speechless and had nothing to say. I was looking at him and Mink was very upset, and the look in his eyes frightened me. I looked up to God and whispered a silent prayer of forgiveness and peace of mind. When I looked back at Mink's face the look was gone, as if I had never seen it in the first place. Mink leaned over kissed me on my cheek, and then he walked back into the house as if everything was all right, like that was a normal conversation between two people. I stood out there for a minute longer thinking about everything that Mink had said to me, and then I said out loud, "God please watch over all of us."

The feeling that I had in the pit of my stomach the other day was back, and it would not go away. I just knew that something bad was about to happen, but I had no idea what it would be. I am not a superstitious person, but something was definitely not right in our auras, and when the shit hit the fan it was going to be an ugly sight. Christmas night I could not get to sleep to save my life. I was sweating and shaking all night long. Shit, I was about to call the ambulance, and just like that the pain went away. If I did not experience that feeling myself, I would not have believed that it took place. I looked up at the ceiling, and said, "This shit is getting out of hand, God."

I took the next two days off from work because I had a lot of running around left to do for Shonda's wedding reception. Never in my life had I seen a person so overjoyed. I had never seen Shonda this happy, except when she gave birth to her son. Michael was so good with Ty, as he wanted to be called ever since Christmas. Ty told us that he was no longer a baby so we had to drop the "little" from his name, and we all respected his wishes. He was getting so big, and he treated Diamond just like his little sister, they were so cute together.

India and I had planned a surprise bachelorette party for Shonda, and it was going to be off the hook. It was going to be fifteen to twenty friends at my house in Queens, and I had hired four male strippers. Their names said it all. There was Midnight, Chocolate Thunder, Billy The Kid, and The Mandingo Warrior. These four brothers had the biggest and blackest dicks that I had ever seen in my life. Shit, they were even bigger then Mink, and he was extra-big. Shonda was going to lose her mind when she saw them. I had a small dinner catered, and Mama Green told me that she would watch the kids so everything was all set to jump off.

The morning of the party, I had the house decorated then went and got my hair and nails done. When I was done I had nothing else to do, so I went home and took a nice relaxing bubble bath. The food would arrive at six thirty, the guests would get there at eight, and the strippers at nine. After my bath I must have dosed off on the couch, because the telephone rang at six and woke me up. It was the catering service, telling me they were on their way. I had just enough time to throw on my clothes, light my blunt from that morning, and try to relax my mind.

When the caterers rang my doorbell at six thirty I was ready to go, and by seven o'clock everything was set up beautifully. India had arrived by then, so we just relaxed and talked until the guests showed up. At seven forty five, India's cousins Mika, Crystal, and Mocha got there. We all went to school together, so they were my girls and I was happy to see them. Eight fifteen came and everyone was there. I had invited fifteen people from Shonda's job, and surprisingly everyone that accepted the invitation showed up.

We all mingled and got to know one another until the bride-to-be made her appearance. When Michael dropped Shonda off at eight thirty, only India and I were in the front of the house. When Shonda walked in, she was asking me who did all the cars belong to. I told her that my neighbors were having a party and they needed some more space. Satisfied with my answer, she said nothing else, and as we stepped into the living room Shonda was saying, "Jazmine, why the hell is all these damn lights off?" When she clicked the light switch everyone yelled, "Surprise!"

Shonda was so shocked that she started to cry right away. When she calmed herself down she spoke to everyone who was there, thanked them for coming, and then she grabbed a plate of food. After she got her food and found a seat she turned to me and asked me about Nina. I reminded her quietly about Nina's curfew. Then I told her that Nina would definitely see her tomorrow afternoon, and after we got that out of the way it was time to party. Shonda received a lot of nice gifts, but I could not wait for the real fun to begin. At nine thirty the doorbell rang. Shonda was already in the kitchen so I asked her to get the door for me.

When she came into the living room, four sex gods in long leather trench coats were carrying her. You would have thought that none of these bitches had ever seen a man before, because they went fucking wild. When The Gold Mine, as they introduced themselves, sat Shonda in her special chair, they dropped their coats and went to work. They gave me their music, which was all Luke and the 2 Live Crew, and they worked their dicks all night. As the night progressed, several of my party guests disappeared into rooms with one or more of The Gold Mine.

I made it clear early in the evening that they could use any room they wanted as long as it was not Diamond's bedroom. You had to be there to see it. Bitches were fucking in the kitchen, on the floor, up against the wall, they were in closets, and in the bathroom. Whoever was in the bathroom first took the tub, and anyone after that used the sink or the toilet to get their groove on. It was a fuck fest but I was not mad at them, shit if I felt like getting some dick I would have fucked one of The Gold Mine too. Shonda said that she was not going to partake in the festivities either. She said that all of her pussy was for Michael, and I was not mad at her either.

The party lasted until 4:00 AM and by then even the strippers were dead tired. When it was all said and done, the only people that were left were Shonda, India, and me. The wedding would not take place until three in the afternoon, so we slept until ten that morning. Shonda asked to borrow my car so that she could take care of some last minute things. She said that she would drop India off at home, and then she would be back for me and Nina by one thirty. I told her not a problem, by then Nina should be here, and then I went back to bed. I spent two more hours under my covers before Nina called and said that she was on her way over.

The day was finally here, Nina's first overnight pass. I was so proud of her, but even better than that she was proud of herself. When she arrived, she looked real relaxed and right away I filled her in on the bachelorette party that she had missed the night before. Then we talked about the good old times that we had together before I met Mink. We talked about all the guys that we had met over the years, and we talked about Wella. We talked about the disease that would eventually take Nina and Mink away from me, and we talked about Mink's trial. Before we knew it, it was one o'clock and the countdown was on, it was finally time to get ready for the wedding.

Shonda got back at one fifteen, and we were just getting dressed. After Nina and Shonda kissed hello, Shonda jumped in the shower, and by one fifty we were on the road to my sister's new life. When we reached the courthouse, Michael was already inside filling out the paperwork. When he noticed us he jumped up and kissed Shonda hard on her lips, like he did not think she was going to show up at all. Shonda asked him what was wrong, and he told her nothing he just needed to feel her against him.

I thought to myself that they were so cute together, and if two people deserved to be happy then it was them. Michael was an only child, and it was just him and his mother. He was very humble, and a straight-up mama's boy, but he was a real good man. Nothing else mattered as long as he treated my sister and nephew with love and respect. If he did that he would always be all right in my book. And as I looked at their faces, all I saw was love and I was proud to be involved in their wedding ceremony. Unknown to Michael, who thought that his mother was not going to be able to attend the reception, Mrs. Bell had already arrived into town from Atlanta.

Mrs. Bell checked into her hotel that morning. She called me right after Nina woke me up. She told me that she had made it here safely, and she would see me later on tonight. Today would be a day of true love and many surprises. When the clerk called Michael and Shonda's names, we all stood up and walked into the chapel with smiles on our faces. When the judge said, "I now pronounce you husband and wife, you may kiss your bride," we were all in tears. Clown-ass Nina had to say some funny shit to lighten the mood. She said, "Ladies and gentlemen, introducing …" Then she did a little dance, and she screamed out, "Mr. and Ms. Michael Bell!"

We laughed all the way outside, and all the way to the parking lot, because homegirl was just too silly for words. Once we reached our vehicles, no one was very hungry, but you could see the lust in Michael and Shonda's eyes. It looked like they were ready to tear each other's clothes off right there in the parking lot. So the newlyweds bid us farewell, and they went on their merry way. Nina and I headed back uptown to my house to change our clothes and get ready for the wedding reception tonight.

We got to Mars 2112 at five that evening. The guests were not scheduled to arrive until seven, so we had two hours to prepare and get everything set up. When we walked in the restaurant, the Greens were already there getting everything together. Nina and I got busy and started helping, and by six everything was finished. Mrs. Bell came through the door at six thirty with bags of presents for her son, new daughter-in-law, and her new grandson. Mink would be bringing Ty and Diamond by at seven thirty, and Michael and Shonda would be here by eight.

Once we finished setting up the place looked beautiful. The color scheme was peach, Shonda's favorite color, and Ivory, Michael's favorite color. These colors represented the true meaning of love for this couple, and I was happy that I was able to be a part of their union. I knew that Shonda would be very happy when she walked in, and that time was rapidly approaching. When Mink brought the children at seven forty five he said hello to me but he seemed very withdrawn, and he headed straight to the open bar. I could not get a handle on Mink's state of mind, but I would worry about that later. Tonight was all about Michael and Shonda. This was their night.

Everyone who was invited had arrived by this time, and then the newlyweds finally came through the door. I could tell that Shonda was overwhelmed when she looked around and saw how everything was arranged. When Michael noticed his mother standing in the corner, he looked like he would faint on the spot. After Mrs. Bell hugged Michael, Shonda, and Ty, Michael looked over at me and whispered, "I love you, Sis, and thanks."

I whispered back, "I love you too," and then I mouthed to him that I would do anything for them.

It was about nine thirty, and the party was in full swing. Everyone was eating, drinking, and having a good time. As I looked around at all the people there I did not see Mink anywhere. I wondered to myself where he had disappeared to without me noticing. I knew that he had a few drinks, and I hoped that he did not get himself into any trouble. Then I told myself Mink was a grown man, and he knew right from wrong. So I pushed my concerns to the side again, and then I continued to get my party on.

At the night wore on everyone was tore up from the floor up, and it felt good. At five seconds to twelve we all gathered around with a drink in our hands, and counted down with the people who were at Times Square. The children stayed until twelve thirty, and then they went home with the Greens, but the rest of us partied until six in the morning. At the end of the night, everywhere I looked people could barely keep their eyes open. The women had their shoes in their hands and the men were looking for misplaced suit jackets and ties. We were a hot mess, but at least everyone was leaving in good sprits.

Nina was fast asleep on the sofa in the corner, and when I woke her up homegirl's hair was a mess. She had danced all night long, and now she was dead tired. When she finally pulled herself together, I asked her if she had seen Mink before she had fell asleep. She said, "Yeah, I did, the last time I saw Mink he was at the bar tossing the drinks back—that had to be hours ago right after the ball dropped." I did not know why I was worried about Mink, but I was. And I knew in my heart that he was gone from my daughter's life once again, and I knew that this time he did not want to be found.

Thank the Lord that we did not have to help do anything; cleanup was included in the fee. So everyone either walked to their cars or they called a cab to take their drunken asses home. Nina did not drink alcohol, so she was not drunk. She drove us back to my place, and when got inside we just crashed. No talking about the night, or anything else, we just needed a bed, quick, fast, and in a hurry. My last thought for the night before I closed my eyes was that the reception was a success, and New Year's Day came in with a hell of a bang.

Chapter Fourteen

Redemption

Right after the New Year came in, my worst fears were confirmed, because once again Mink had disappeared from our lives. Two months had passed, and no one had seen or heard from him since the night of Michael and Shonda's reception. The Greens were very worried, so they filed another missing person's report. Detectives Munch and Terry were on the case once again, and once again they still had no leads. Diamond was growing up fast, and she was a beautiful little girl who looked just like her father. She was always asking about her daddy, and once again I did not know what to tell her.

Ty was happy because Shonda was four months pregnant, and he was going to be a big brother again. Michael could not wait to be a father, and Mrs. Bell could not wait to be a grandmother again. Nina was progressing well in the program, and soon she would be released into an outpatient program. All around me there was love and hope being spread, giving people the impression that life could get better. I tried to believe in love, but how could I feel that way after all that I had been through?

I felt like Mink did in on our last conversation on Christmas Day—very overwhelmed. Shit, I needed a vacation just to get away from my life. I needed to get to know me, but now was not the appropriate time for me to be thinking about running away. With Mink missing in action, and no leads on his case, I needed to be around for Diamond and the Greens. I was trying to be strong for everyone else, but who would be strong for me. Working for Doctor Okonkwo was the only sense of peace that I had. She was so encouraging, and in a lot of ways I guess she was what I needed. I needed a shining light over this dark cloud that seemed to keep following me all over the place.

Doctor Okonkwo came to work one day and told me about a vision that she had the night before. She started off by saying, "Jazmine, there are some things that I need to tell you about myself. You can hear me out, and take what I am saying with a grain of salt, or you can disregard what I am about to tell you. Either way I have to tell it to you, and you have to listen. Back in my homeland of Africa, some people believed that my grandmother was a witch. I don't know, maybe she was or she was not. All I do know is that she had visions about people that always came true.

"Now people also say that this gift passes down through generations. I know that my mother did not have the gift, but I do. Now you can believe me or not, but I need to tell you what I saw. Last night my vision was about, you and Jonathon."

I said, "Doctor Okonkwo, how do you know my daughter's father's real name? I have never told it to you."

She said, "Jazmine, it was in my vision last night." Then she said, "Jonathon is going through some very hard times right now, and he needs your help."

I interrupted her again and said, "Oh my God Doctor Okonkwo, Jonathon has been missing since New Year's Day."

She looked at me and said, "Yes, Jazmine, I know, now please let me finish my story. Jazmine, drugs have become a very big part of Jonathon's life."

I was sitting there in shock. I said, "Doctor Okonkwo you must be mistaken. Jonathon does not do drugs, he has never indulged in any drug substance before."

Then she looked at me and said, "Jazmine, I am never mistaken. He is using any drug that he can get his hands on, thinking that it will take his pain away. And he is dealing with some very shady people who are out to hurt him.

"He is using heroin, crack, angel dust, and cocaine. If you do not save him soon, you will never see Jonathon alive again. Jazmine, Jonathon has been on 127th Street and Lenox Avenue in building one twenty. He is in the apartment on the top floor, and he has been there for the last two weeks. Jazmine, Jonathon really wants to get help but he also needs you in his life. I don't know what went wrong between you two, but I know in my heart that you still love him. There is no problem that big that it will make you turn your back on the one you love.

"You must always remember that love conquers all. Just think about what I said, and if you need sometime off from work just let me know. You are a very sweet person, and I want you to have the best out of life." Then she walked away, looked back, and said, "Now get your butt back to work."

All I could do was smile; Doctor Okonkwo sure had a way with words. I sat there and tried to do my work for the rest of the day, but work did not come easily to me.

Mink was on my mind all day, and when I picked Diamond up from the day care center, her first words out of her month were, "Mommy, I want my daddy." Just like that my mind was made up, and I knew what I had to do. I was going to get my man.

That day was Friday, so I called Mama Green and asked her if Diamond could spend the weekend over there with them. She told me that was fine, and to bring her over. I was glad that Diamond had clothes over there, because going home was out of the question. When I dropped my daughter off I gave her a kiss and told her that I would see her real soon. Then I was off on my journey to save Mink.

On the ride to Manhattan I prayed to God for guidance and strength to see me through this ordeal. I hoped that Mink was still in that building when I got there, but I was scared about what I would find. When I reached my destination a calmness came over me, and I was suddenly at peace. This was a feeling that I had never experienced before, and I knew that God was right there walking with me. When I reached the building I took a deep breath and then wanted until someone opened the door. I stood there for five minutes, and then a man came walking out and I walked right in.

The elevator was there so I walked on, and it seemed to take the longest time to get to the sixth floor. When the doors opened I was hoping that Mink was still inside the apartment, and that my boss was right about her vision. When I got to the only door on the floor, someone was just coming out of the apartment. I was not sure if it was a man or a women, so I called out, "Excuse me, but do you know Mink?" It looked up at me wide-eyed, as if it did not see me standing there when it first walked out the door.

Then with a squeaky voice it said, "Yeah, he's in the back."

I thanked whatever that was, and then I walked inside the door. I could not believe the condition that this apartment was in, it looked real bad. All the lights in the house was turned off, and that crack smell was thick in the air. All I could do was yell out Mink's name, and hope that he answered me. After about five minutes of me calling out Mink's name, a dark figure started coming toward me. All I heard was, "Jazmine, is that you?"

When my eyes adjusted to the darkness, I could not believe my eyes. It was Mink, but he did not look like himself at all. He had lost so much weight that he looked like a skeleton. He had on clothing five sizes too big, and he had on some big Ronald McDonald-type shoes on his feet.

I said, "Yes, Mink, it's me, now let's go home."

"Jazmine, you don't want me to come home with you, so please just leave me alone."

"No, Mink, I will not leave you alone, I came here to get you and I am not leaving without you."

"Jazmine, what can I do for you or Diamond? I can't do shit for you, so just leave me the fuck alone."

I took a deep breath, and then I said, "Mink, it's not what you can do for us, it's what we can do for you."

He looked away and then he said, "Jazmine, I'm going to die. I have AIDS, remember?"

I walked toward him and said, "Well if you come home with me at least you can die with some dignity, and you will have redemption." Mink looked at me clearly for the first time that evening, and started walking toward the door. We took the elevator downstairs, and with his head down he headed straight to the car.

The ride home was tense. Mink kept tweaking and it was driving me fucking crazy. I guess he tried his best to stay still, but he just could not. He cut the radio on but the music seemed to make him nervous, so he cut it back off. Then he rolled the window down, because out of nowhere beads of sweat started rolling down his face. But when I looked back over at him, he was shaking like he was freezing so then he rolled the window back up.

The next thing I know he was taking off his clothes, so I pulled over to the side of the road shut the engine off and looked at him. I said, "Mink, I can't take this shit anymore, you have to pull yourself together at least until we get home. The only way that this is going to work is if you want it to."

He looked at me and said real low, "I want it to work, Jazmine."

I said, "Okay, Mink, then make it work." The rest of the ride home was quiet; we were both deep in our own thoughts. Mink tried the best that he could to stay still, and we made it home without any further incident. When we got to the house, I led Mink straight to the bathroom, and stripped him naked. I turned on the water, and washed him like he was a newborn baby.

After his shower I asked was he hungry, and he told me no but I made him some soup and crackers to eat anyway. As we were sitting there on the bed, he was nodding off so I told him to go ahead and lay down. By the time that I left the room, he was already fast asleep. I went to the living room and laid down on the couch, and when I opened my eyes it was the next morning. I checked on Mink and he was still fast asleep, so I ran to the supermarket up the block to get some groceries.

I did not know how much food we would need, so I just started grabbing everything in sight. I got a lot of liquids, so he wouldn't get dehydrated, and I got a lot of sweets, because I knew that he would be craving them, and I was back in the house within the hour. When I got back to the house I put the food away, and then I called Mama Green. I asked her could Diamond stay over there for a few more days, and then I explained to her the situation with Mink. She was relieved to know that he was safe and sound. Then she told me to keep on praying, and to take all the time that I needed. After we spoke for a minute longer, I spoke to my baby girl. I told her that Mommy had to go away for a week for my job, but I would be back soon.

Diamond said to me, "Okay, Mommy," and then she told me that she loved me very much. I told her that I loved her too, and then Mama Green came back on the line. I told her that I would keep in touch, and after that we hung up. For the next five days all Mink wanted to do was sleep and eat sweets. He was sweating, shaking, screaming, hollering, vomiting, and shitting, and there was nothing that I could do about it. I could not help him with withdrawal from the drugs, and at night it only seemed to get worse.

Mink was hanging on by a single string, and then on the sixth day everything seemed to subside, just like that. I heard Mink moving around upstairs that morning, so I started cooking us breakfast. When he came downstairs he was already dressed, clean shaven, and he looked like the old Mink, only thinner. That day we bonded, and I made a promise to him. Mink told me that he did not want to die without me and Diamond by his side. He said that he needed his family in his life to survive. And with tears in my eyes, I promised him from that day forth that he would have his family back in his life forever

Two weeks had passed, and Mink was finally strong enough to go outside and get some air. I knew that he had not been to see a doctor in awhile, so Monday morning we would walk into the clinic. Over the next couple of days Mink slept a lot, but I knew that he needed to get his strength back, so I left him alone. On that following Monday we ate a light breakfast, and then we set out bright and early. By the time we arrived there it was eight thirty, and the clinic was already crowded. I knew that it was going to be a long and tiring day.

We were at the clinic for about five hours, Mink had to fill out a lot of paperwork, and the nurses drew a lot of blood samples from him. Once that was done we had to wait awhile for the results, after another hour had passed the doctor finally called us into his office. The doctor told us that Mink had really abused his body with all the drugs that he had taken.

Over the last few months a lot of damage had been done to Mink's organs, and now the disease was in its final stage. The doctor told us that Mink had about three to six months left on this earth, and there was nothing that we could do about it. I cried in Mink's arms for a very long time. But Mink said that he wanted to make the best of the little bit of time that he had left, and that he just wanted to enjoy his family. So I wiped my tears and put on my game face. I would be strong for him and I needed to be strong for Diamond.

When we left the doctor's office, we went straight to his parent's house. When Diamond saw her daddy two days before her birthday she was beyond happy. After he played with our daughter for a little while, he asked Miracle to take her upstairs so that the grown-ups could talk. Then he sat down and he explained to his parents what the doctor just told us. His mother cried, and his father just looked sick to his stomach. We all knew that this would be the last birthday that Mink would celebrate with Diamond, so we made it a big affair.

We had the party at the Green's house, and all the family was there. Nina was finally out of the program also. She had a job as a receptionist downtown, and she was living in Wella's old apartment in the projects. I asked her why she didn't come and stay with me when she got out? She told me that she needed her own space and that I needed my own space. She said that she had to do this on her own, or else she would never stay clean.

She also said that she joined a support group called P. L.W.A. The letters stood for People Living With AIDS. They went around twice a week to different schools, hospitals, churches, and anywhere else to spread HIV awareness so that people would not end up like them, fighting a never ending battle. Nina and her group were spreading the only cure for HIV that we had—always wear a condom, always get to know your partner, and always get tested. She was very positive about what she was doing, and I was happy that she was so happy.

As I looked over my shoulder, Shonda was walking over to us, and she had a big plate of food in her hands. Her stomach had gotten so big that she looked like she was a watermelon about to explode. The whole night all Shonda did was eat and eat, while Michael ran back and forth like a chicken with his head cut off. But he did not mind, trust me brother man was in love.

Diamond had a ball, and she wore her little self out by the end of her birthday party. By the time we got home she was out for the count, so I just put on her pajamas and tucked her into bed. That was the first night that

Mink and I laid together as a man and a woman in a long time, and you know what it felt good.

We knew that sex was out of the question between us, but it felt good just to be held and touched by the only man that I ever really loved. Mink said that he would never have intercourse with me because when he died I would have to be here to take care of our daughter. He said that we could not depend on condoms, and I agreed with him. As the weeks wore on, you could tell that the disease was starting to take over his body, but Mink would not let it win. He took Diamond to school every day, picked her up, cooked breakfast, lunch, and dinner, and he washed the clothes.

He did anything and everything that needed to be done around the house. He said that he had to stay busy and moving around kept him from thinking about dying. On June 20, 2002, Shonda gave birth to an eight-pound, ten-ounce baby boy they named Michael Justin Bell II. He was the cutest thing that you ever saw, and he was so fat just like a turkey. Life was finally good for us, and my family was even better.

Chapter Fifteen

The Beginning Before the End

Mink woke up refreshed the morning after Shonda had the baby. He said that before he got to sick to leave the house, he wanted me to become his wife. So we had a small ceremony at his parent's house that weekend, surrounded by family and friends. Diamond was the prettiest flower girl that you ever saw, and Ty was a handsome ring bearer. Mink's brothers—Reggie, Man Man, and Michael—were his groomsmen, and Shonda, Nina, and India were my bridesmaids. Miracle was a junior bridesmaid, and Pop Green gave me away.

It was a beautiful service, and when it was over I was very happy. I finally got to wear my white dress. The bridesmaid's dresses were a soft burgundy, and all the men had on white tuxedos with burgundy cummerbunds. Everything was so magical, and at last the minister said those familiar words, only this time he was talking about me. "Ladies and gentlemen, I am proud to introduce to you Mr. and Ms. Jonathon Mink Green."

We did not have a big reception like Shonda and Michael, but it was still very nice. Of course Mama Green cooked all the food, so you know that the food was off the hook, and there was nothing left over at the end of the reception. After our wedding we settled into married life well. It was no different then before, except now my last name was Green.

August first was the first time that I noticed how gaunt Mink's face had become. He was only weighing about one hundred and ten pounds, and he was getting smaller by the second. Getting up every day was a hard task for Mink, so mostly he just stayed in our bedroom. On Mink's weekly doctor's appointment we were told that it was only a matter of time now. He told Mink to just take it easy, and he told me to stay by Mink's side.

At first Diamond did not understand why her daddy was so sick. I tried to explain it to her the best way that I could. But no matter what I told her, all she wanted to do was sit by his side, hold his hand, and sing to him. A few days later she told me that she knew that her daddy would die soon, and then she told me that she understood a lot more then I thought she did.

Children are funny that way. Adults could not handle this kind of sorrow, but Diamond wore her sorrow on her shirtsleeve. She told me that she would be a big girl, and that she was not going to cry. She said that her daddy would be in a better place real soon, and then she gave me a kiss and went to watch her cartoons.

Nina stopped by every two days just to sit and talk with Mink. In some ways, she blamed herself that he was dying from AIDS. She said that working with P.L.W.A made it a little easier for her, and this was her way of giving back to Mink just by being by his side. Of course the Greens came by everyday, and Mink's mother just sat and prayed for him. His father just looked real sad knowing that his son's days on this earth were numbered.

The first week of his parents coming over Mink accepted the Lord Jesus Christ as his personal savior, so when he finally departed from this earth Mink would be going home to heaven. When Mink passed away he would be going home to see his heavenly father, and he would be allowed to enter into the pearly gates. I was so happy that Mink had finally made peace with himself.

Shonda and Michael came over one weekend, and they brought the children for a visit. It was really nice seeing them, and Diamond was so happy to have someone to play with. I cooked spaghetti for dinner, and then the kids and I played monopoly. Mink slept most of that day, and it seemed that he was always so very tired. He was sinking into himself right before my eyes, and he was literally drained of all his energy.

The only bright spot in my life was that my twenty-fifth birthday was in two days, and Nina, Shonda, and India said that we were going out to celebrate. Mama Green already said that she would come over and sit with Mink and Diamond while I was gone, so the plan was all set. I really did not want to go out and have a good time. Not while Mink was at home dying, but Mink felt that I needed to get out of the house, so I finally agreed to go.

The next two days were very long for my family, Mink could not make it to the bathroom on his own, and so he had quite a few accidents. But he still held his head up high, and he did not give up his faith. He said that he knew he was dying, but he was going to die like a man.

On August sixth my birthday we were all going to meet up at Shonda's house, just to have a few drinks and chill before we went out to eat. When I arrived at Shonda's that evening India and Nina were already there, so I had to play catch-up with the drinks to feel as good as they were feeling. Nina was the only one not drinking, but she was still happy to be alive, and honey was ready to get her eat on.

After my second drink of Absolute, Shonda suggested that we leave her house and hit the road. We were going to Red Lobster in Bay Plaza in the Bronx, and that place always had an extra-long wait for a table. When we got there, just like I thought they told us that it would be a forty-five minute wait, so you know that we headed straight to the bar to continue our party. Shonda, India, and I had two drinks apiece, while Nina had orange juice, and thirty minutes later our name was finally called.

As we went to follow our waitress I noticed a group of females watching us. I did not know why they were staring, but I did not know them so I thought nothing else of it. We stayed in Red Lobster for over three hours, and when we left our stomachs were extra full. As we walked to the door to leave I noticed the same group of females watching us, and then they started walking toward the door right behind us.

I tapped India on her shoulder and I asked her if she knew the girls. She looked at them and said no. India said that she had never seen them a day in her life. When I looked in front of me Shonda and Nina were heading into the bathroom, and by the time they came back out I had forgotten all about our female watchers.

Shonda's car was parked around the corner from Red Lobster, and we could not wait to get back downtown to her house to relax. The ride home was full of laughter, and Nina was cracking jokes as usual. I guess that was why none of us noticed the dark blue Toyota following behind us. Life is funny sometimes, just when you think your life has taken a turn for the better, the devil is always working overtime to mess everything up.

Somehow I knew that this was the beginning before the end, and everything that happened after we left the restaurant seemed totally unreal. If it did not happen to me I would not have believed it, and it all happened just like we were in a fucked-up movie. Everything was moving in slow motion, and I wish that I had remembered to ask Nina and Shonda about those bitches that were watching us inside the restaurant.

Shonda pulled up in front of the building, and she parked the car just as my cell phone rang out. As I was getting out of the car, I looked down at the screen, and saw my home number. I took a deep breath, but I already knew in my heart that something was terribly wrong with Mink. And as I pressed the talk button on my phone, I heard a female voice behind me say, "You bitches thought that shit was over with, right?"

As I said hello, all I heard was Mama Green crying. She said, "Jazmine, he's leaving us, baby." She cleared her throat, and then she said that Mink needed to hear my voice one last time before he took his last breath. When she said those words, that was the moment that I heard the first gunshot.

Mama Green put Mink on the phone, and when I said hello the first bullet hit me in my side. Mink said, "Jazmine, I'm dying baby," and then the second shot hit me in my lower back. Mink said, "I will always love you, Jazmine, and I never meant to hurt you."

I told him that I loved him too, and then he coughed and the line got very quiet. At that moment I knew that Mink was dead, and I would never see his face ever again. All around me all I heard was screaming, but for some reason I could not figure out was going on.

The next thing I heard was Shonda saying, "Jazmine, hold on baby, the ambulance is on its way."

Then I heard Nina say, "No, Jazmine, don't close your eyes, baby." But I had to close my eyes because I saw Mink and he was holding out his hand to me telling me to come on.

"Come on, Jazmine, he's waiting for us," said Mink.

I asked him, "Mink who's waiting for us?"

Then he laughed and said, "Silly, Jesus is waiting for us."

I heard Shonda saying, "Jazmine, repent of your sins, and take the Lord as your personal savior." She kept saying, "Come on, Jazmine, open up your eyes, please."

I opened my eyes and saw Shonda and Nina kneeling over me, and they were crying. All I had time to say was, "God forgive me for my sins, and yes I want to make it into heaven."

Then I closed my eyes again, only this time it would be forever. From far away I heard Shonda and Nina screaming, "Jazmine, please don't die," but I had no other choice.

Didn't they know that Mink was waiting for me on the other side, and that God was waiting for us? But all I kept thinking was, what about Diamond who would watch out for her? Then Mink looked at me and said, "Don't worry, our little girl will be just fine." I asked him how did he know, and he asked me just to trust him.

Then I said, "I just don't want to hurt anymore."

Mink grabbed my hand and said to me, "Don't worry baby, you won't." Then we walked into paradise together. At 11:35 PM on August 6, 2002, Jonathon Mink Green, and Jazmine Marie Roberts Green went home to meet their creator as one.

Epilogue

The Light At the End
Of the Rainbow

Life is funny sometimes. Yes it did take the police a whole lot of time. And yes, it did take a lot more effort then they are used to, but eventually they did find out who killed me on a quiet street in Harlem. It took them all of two months to get enough evidence on my case, but when they got it the person responsible for my murder was arrested that same day. My family would learn her name two days after her arrest, and then everything would make a lot of sense. Her name was Tamiko, and she was the older sister of big Ty's baby mother Latrell.

The word on the street was that the dumb bitch was running around bragging about killing me. But she should have known that the street don't love nobody, and it sure wasn't anybody's friend. But this is why I said that life is funny sometimes, would you believe that the person responsible for my murder would turn out to be my half sister? Close your damn mouth; my family was just as shocked as you are right now. But yes it's true. Tamiko and I carried the same blood running through our veins.

We shared the same father, Bernard J. Perkins. All of this information came out at her trial, and it came from Bernard's sister and me, and Tamiko's aunt Shelia. She was my father's younger sister, and she knew all about my mother and the rape that produced me. She told my family all of this one day while they were sitting outside waiting while the court was on lunch. She told them that at one time she was out there in the streets with my parents getting high too. They were all running in the same circles, but after her mother and brother's death, she decided to change her life around.

My grandmother Lucy had left a life insurance policy in Shelia's name for a large amount of money, and because her mother died she was able to live. Shelia then told them that she got the money and went straight into a drug treatment program to get clean. She was away for two and a half years but when she came home she had a new apartment, money, and a new lease in life. She knew that there was a light at the end of the rainbow, and she was going to grab a hold of it. Then my aunt told them that Tamiko and I were born in the same year, and that we were three months apart.

Shelia said that she tried to contact my mother several times in the past so that she could come and see me. She said that my mother always turned her away, and after awhile she just stopped trying. She said that she always kept in touch with Tamiko, and her mother Denise over the years. Denise met my sick, perverted father around the same time as my mother Tracey.

Shelia said that she tried to tell Tamiko about me over the years, but Tamiko told her that I was not her damn sister, and that she did not want to meet me ever. I guess she met me anyway, because she turned out to be the cause of my demise.

One week after her trial started, Tamiko was found guilty on all charges. She was sentenced to twenty-five years to life with no possibility of parole for my murder, and my friend's attempted murder. Tamiko's young life was over, and she had to live with the knowledge that she killed her half sister. India was also wounded that night. She was shot once in the right leg but the bullet went straight through and she was fine in no time at all.

Our funeral was a real home-going service fit for a king and queen. God says weep not but rejoice in the Lord, and that's just what they did. We were laid to rest in matching white caskets, and we were also wearing all white. Mink had on his white Armani suit, and I had on a flowing white Armani dress. We looked just like angels, and the best part is that we made it into paradise together.

Shonda and Michael got custody of our precious baby girl Diamond, but the Greens could see her anytime that their heart's desired. Diamond was surrounded by love, and even though her parents were taken away from her to soon she felt the love that we had for her. Nina Gonzalez, my best friend in the whole wide world, lived ten more wonderful years, and she was the best godmother that any child could ever have.

Mink and I have watched over Diamond all of these years, and Shonda and Michael have given her a good life. When we first died Diamond was very withdrawn, and it took her a while to shake off the pain of losing us. She was very sad at our home-going service, but my boss, Doctor Okonkwo, came and gave her a very special gift. It was a charm bracelet with a man and a woman on it.

She told Diamond that it was her new good luck charm, and as long as she kept it close to her heart her mommy and daddy would always be with her. And as I am looking down on my daughter right now, ten years later, Diamond still has us close to her heart. I want you to always remember after reading my story, that sometimes the choices that we make in life will lead us around different circles. Some of them good and some of them bad, but always remember that the choice is yours. So choose wisely, hold your head up, and you might just prevail.

Circles

Things have happened in my life
Which have me depressed
Just wanting to be out of sight
Hiding out in a world all my own
Where my fear won't be able to be shown
Wanting to be left alone
All people want to do is console

Not wanting to open up
Keeping my feelings locked away deep inside
Where I have the key and there is no escape
Pleading for someone to help
The pain is all in my eyes
But no one seems to see
All they seem to do is look through me

Knowing the pain that I feel
But choosing to look away
I'm hiding in a world which is all my own
No exit, no escape just wanting to run far away

You understand what I feel
Because in your heart you have felt the same
Wanting and wishing to start a new day
But I am too ashamed and I always feel so afraid

What would my life be like, if I were to just go away?
To a faraway place where I won't feel any pain
No shame, no disgrace, no feeling sorry for myself
Never feeling alone, and never having to cry out for help
Helping myself the way I wanted another to do
Taking back control of my life
And just making it through

The End

Printed in the United States
by Baker & Taylor Publisher Services